BILLIONAIRES, BULLETS, EXPLODING MONKEYS

Also by Mike Attebery
On/Off – A Jekyll & Hyde Story
Seattle On Ice

BILLIONAIRES, BULLETS, EXPLODING MONKEYS

by

Mike Attebery

Cryptic Bindings
Seattle, Washington

Cryptic Bindings
Seattle, Washington
Billionaires, Bullets, Exploding Monkeys

Cryptic Bindings
Visit our website at www.crypticbindings.com
Read Mike Attebery's Blog: www.mikeattebery.com

Second Edition: April 2012

ISBN 978-0-615-59143-8

Publisher's Note:
This is a work of fiction. Names, characters, places, and incidents are either the product of the author's imagination or are used fictitiously, any resemblance to actual persons (living or dead), business establishments, events, or locales is coincidental.

Printed in the United States of America.

If you ever had a job you hated, this book is for you.

NICK

Someone on the bus stank. It was unbearable, like a moldy washcloth, buried under a sink full of dishes. Nick knew the smell well. Lately it seemed he only got around to cleaning the kitchen once a month, if that. He used to be obsessive about it, but then he'd started screwing around with Morgan, which meant he ate all his meals on the run and was never home. They never came back to his place; his conscience would have killed him.

He was a married man, cheating on his wife with a college sophomore. He felt terrible about what he was doing, but at the same time, it didn't feel entirely wrong. Yeah, he was married, but it sure as hell didn't feel like he was, and as far as most people knew, he wasn't. In the last year, he and his wife had been together only once, for what had been a less than cozy week. He wasn't sure what the deal was. It was like Kendra was two different people. There was the girl he'd met as a senior at the University -- that Kendra had been funny, spontaneous, and a bit of a freak, the good kind of freak, the bedroom variety. They'd had a good sex life, a good relationship, never a boring one. That Kendra was exciting, and intense, and present, always present. Her eyes were always on him, reading his thoughts, smiling oddly when she caught him looking her way.

Then they'd gotten married.

That was her idea.

At the time they'd been together about seven months, which was short, but something about their relationship had seemed different somehow. Destiny or what have you. She brought up the idea, he couldn't think of a reason not to, so they'd gone for it. Kendra handled the wedding stuff while Nick planned the honeymoon. He booked them a room at the Olympic Hotel downtown, a Seattle classic with just enough New York snoot to make Kendra swoon. They'd stayed there for one weekend, fucking their brains out, lazing around the room, and wandering the town, goo-goo-eyed and dreamy. In the fall they found an apartment in Greenlake and Kendra started her graduate work at the college.

Meanwhile, Nick had gone about trying to put his liberal arts degree to work. That was easier said than done. He wanted to be a writer, movies mostly, books maybe, but the thing was, people didn't go around hiring fiction writers. Hell, they didn't seem to hire anybody. He and Kendra had been fortunate enough to graduate during the worst job market in years. Course, Kendra had planned on grad school from the start. He'd always had a chip on his shoulder when it came to going back to school. College was more fun for fictional inspiration than for living.

Despite his troubles finding work, that summer had been fun. Kendra still had her student worker position at the college through the fall, and a bunch of Nick's buddies, including Will

Baker, had stayed in the area for a few more nostalgic months. The bunch of them had run around town like old times, drinking and fighting and earning a buck here and there doing demolition and home painting work for Will's father. It was a good summer. Married life seemed to be off on the right foot.

Then came the fall, which brought opportunities for Kendra, and frustrations for Nick.

Kendra was in the graduate program in the School of Oceanography, the same department she'd studied in for her undergrad years. The leap to the Master's program had unleashed a wave of study and research possibilities. As Nick scoured the Net for job postings and rode the bus downtown to deliver countless resumes and personalized cover letters door-to-door, Kendra started coming home with ever-growing piles of research program literature, all of which seemed to involve long stretches of time out on the open water, plenty of sun-drenched tropical locales, and thousands upon thousands of miles separating her from Seattle, and him. They'd just signed a one-year lease, and Nick was dead broke, but no matter how he tried to reason with her, he knew Kendra was dying to take part in one of the studies. He didn't know what worried him. Maybe it was the newlywed thing. Maybe it was just jealousy. He was having a hard time, she was having a ball. Whatever it was, he told himself he was being petty, they'd made the commitment to each other. They were married. Wasn't this what marriage was all about? She'd do her thing while he made the sacrifice and stayed in Seattle. In the future his own work might take him from the area, and then she'd return the favor, either traveling with him, or making things work at home while he followed opportunity wherever it might lead.

"It's not that important. Other projects will come up," she muttered.

"Are you sure?" he asked, leaning his head down to look her in the eyes.

She'd turned, "Of course."

He'd sat there quietly. He could still remember the sound of the heater kicking on in the next room. The bubbles rumbling up through the radiator pipes.

"Go," he said. "You have to go."

"I don't *have* to," she protested, but the way she said "have" told him that she did.

So, she'd applied. He'd insisted on it.

The letter of acceptance arrived in October, but that had been a mere formality. Kendra had interviewed with only current and former professors from the University, so her admission was a done deal. The middle of fall was a blur. By Thanksgiving, all of Nick's buddies had left town, and Kendra had her tickets in hand to go to Key West for the next nine months. She'd be back in the summer, and every chance she could get before then. Kendra had made their Thanksgiving dinner, then the next day they'd celebrated Christmas, eating leftover turkey and exchanging their presents in case they couldn't afford airline tickets for the actual holiday when it did come around. On Sunday night Nick drove her to the airport, they kissed goodbye, and she got on the plane.

That was when the second Kendra had slowly made her debut. When she first got to Florida, the calls had been frequent. She told him about the program, about the scientists, about the other researchers. She was getting her diving certification, learning the area, getting settled in. Then, slowly but surely, the calls had begun to taper off. She'd promise to call at a certain time, then she wouldn't. He'd call, get her voice mail, then finally hear from her, sounding distracted or tired, or just plain detached. He'd somehow brushed that off as his own insecurity. He still hadn't found a regular gig and was working as a temp in the customer service department for Starbucks Corporate. The job was hell. He came home at night, six-pack in hand, opening the first bottle even as he walked to the fridge to deposit the carrier. Sitting at home, drunk, in an empty apartment, he began to grow suspicious. Why wasn't she calling? He'd sit there and stew, clasping his hands together, digging his fingers into the seat cushions as he considered the possibilities, every possible indiscretion flickering through his mind. Then, occasionally, she'd call and he'd feel a little bit better.

She finally made it back for a visit in March. It was an awkward reunion. He met her at the airport and felt an immediate chill. It didn't seem so much like she didn't want to be there, as it seemed she was too busy to relax and spend the time with him. His heart had fluttered when he first caught sight of her coming down the concourse at Seatac. *Fluttered!* There was no manly word for it. He was glad to see her. The last few months had been dreary. She looked great. He waved, she smiled slightly, and he leaned in to kiss her. Looking back on it, he had to lean in just a bit too far, but as with everything else, he ignored it.

"Hey. I've missed you," He said.

She brushed the hair from her eyes and looked up. "I've

missed you too."

As soon as she said it, he knew she didn't mean it.

The frost melted away slowly during that week, and on the second-to-last night they'd finally made love. It didn't go so well, but they had done it. Perhaps they'd both felt that drastic action was called for. Maybe. Or maybe they'd just wanted a break from asking the same questions.

"Is something wrong?"

"No. Is something wrong with you?"

"No..."

He hated to say it, but Nick was almost relieved when she left. He didn't hear from her for another two weeks. Then she just called to tell him that one of the professors had spoken to a friend in the Department of Immunology at the University, and had put in a good word for him for an Editor of Research Publications position that had opened up. He didn't want the job, but he called, and a week later, he got it.

There wasn't much to say about research papers. He wasn't a scientist. His interests were women, writing, movies, and fiction, in that order. The idea of someone spending their days stabbing mice with syringes and measuring every fluid, growth, and body function that resulted, seemed like a slow death sentence, and not just for the mice. But if he thought that was bad, reading the papers on each study was immeasurably worse. None of the researchers spoke English as their first language, and since scientific lingo was about as understandable to him as a Chinese encyclopedia, he may as well have been reading each manuscript upside down while trying to correct the grammar. His eyes crossed, his mind wandered, and he found himself sinking into his chair each day, glancing at the second hand on the clock, or staring into the wall of his cubicle.

That had all changed in August. The summer, like the rest of the past year, had been quiet. There was a drought in Seattle, so any time outside had been dry, almost blistering. He rode the bus to the University, did his job, good, bad, he didn't know, didn't care. Then he rode the bus home in the sweltering heat, or put on shorts in the men's room and walked home to the apartment in Greenlake, where the night was spent on the couch, staring into the flickering blue glow of the television screen. Kendra phoned about once a month now. August 10th was the date of her last call. She'd been scheduled to return to Seattle around the fifteenth, but had called to discuss the possibility of staying on in the Keys for another year. Nick mumbled something and hung up the phone. He went into work the next day and bumped into Morgan.

She was gorgeous. Kendra was gorgeous, but Morgan had something else, something he couldn't put his finger on. It wasn't that she was flighty, or flirty, though the second term seemed to apply. It was that she was aggressive, and she was *sexy*. If Kendra was Ingrid Bergman, then Morgan was Grace Kelly. Both were classically beautiful women, but one was colder, more reserved, while the other let her interests simmer closer to the surface, where every so often they could boil over and burn you. He knew something would happen between them the first time he saw her. Her eyes told him so. The way she touched him on the shoulder only confirmed it. She was interviewing for a student assistant position in the department. It was about a month before she'd be starting her sophomore year, but she'd come in early to try to beat out the competition. It worked. Afterward, as she stood outside the department conference room, waiting for the manager and one of the professors who had interviewed her to make their decision, she'd wandered down to Nick's cubicle and leaned against the wall, staring at him.

"Hi," she said.

He turned to her with a start. "Hi."

"You work here?"

His faced flushed. "Yeah."

"Are you a student?"

Why was he so nervous?

"I was. I graduated last year."

Her eyes narrowed. "Why are you working here?"

"That's a good question," he sighed.

She laughed.

Then he leaned back in his chair, not sure what to say next. His eyes kept moving down to her chest. He felt like a cartoon wolf. He locked on her eyes as he watched her play with her hair.

"You're interviewing for the assistant job?"

"Yeah."

"You in this program?"

"God no!"

He laughed. "Good."

Then she turned to him. "So are you single or what?"

He almost said, "Excuse me?!" But instead of showing surprise at her sudden question, he listened curiously to his own response.

"It's complicated."

She looked at him and smiled.

"Complicated's okay. Complicated's kind of sexy."

She got the job, and they started hanging out after work. When classes started she took him to parties at her friends' houses. By that time they were more than just friends. They fooled around in the bathrooms at the parties. They went to Morgan's apartment and he stayed the night. He would have felt guilty about what he was doing, but Kendra never called, and whenever he tried her phone, his calls just went to voice mail. Aside from one brief break in November, when the guilt had finally caught up with him and he'd tried to put an end to things, he and Morgan had been fucking like maniacs for the better part of eight months. They'd even started fooling around at work. They'd find handicapped bathrooms with locking doors, the empty offices of professors on sabbatical, they'd even done it in a lecture auditorium after one of Morgan's evening classes. Every time Nick decided it was time to end things, he'd find himself alone with her, and before he knew it, *ending* the affair was the last thing on his mind.

This morning he was feeling a tinge of remorse. He wondered if he was self-destructing because of the job. Lord knew he hated it. Maybe he was getting back at his wife. By now he was certain she was cheating on him too, but with one of the researchers in Florida. Hell, he didn't know what to think. He didn't even know if he was doing a decent job when it came to his editing work. Probably not. He couldn't keep his eyes focused on anything he was reading. It was all mind numbing. Pointless. He tried to burn through the pages as quickly as possible, marking up the visible mistakes and checking things over as best he could, all the while waiting for Morgan to come in for the day and sneak off with him at lunch, or during his first break, or even earlier if he couldn't wait that long. Was anyone onto them? Probably. He didn't even care.

Now here he was, sitting on the bus, riding into work with some body odor lab specimen somewhere in his vicinity. He hated B.O., it made him want to punch people. Today was a big day for the department; someone big was coming in to check up on his grant money. This was Seattle, the software capital of the world. Apparently one of the original computer legends had called that week to set up an appointment. Third richest man in the world, tens of billions of dollars, unmatched influence and power, and yet, Nick wasn't interested in meeting the guy, he just needed his girl, a distraction from the questions in his head, and the quiet of his empty apartment. He just wanted to get to the next stop, get off the bus, get away from the stench, and get to his girl. He had to see Morgan. If it didn't happen soon he was going to scream.

RENOIR

He had five children. Ten grandchildren. Two houses. Two countries. One wife. They'd been married for forty-five years. Isabelle. That was how he categorized his life, if he ever stopped to think about it. To some, the clean, mathematical numbers might have seemed odd, but he'd worked with numbers all his life. He recognized them, processed them without thought. He was a scientist and a professor. When he wasn't performing studies and calculating data, he was teaching courses and determining grades. He liked teaching, as much as he liked anything. His hobby was cooking, a source of constant frustration, but somehow it relaxed him. He was that kind of man. Irritation kept him going. Cooking, like science, required careful measurement, replication of processes, weighing the outcome, and evaluating the results. Michel Renoir was nothing if not methodical. Some thought him odd, others kind. No one would have called him eccentric. At the moment, he was sixty-seven years old.

He woke at 6:30 every day, even on weekends. Today he'd been up at the usual time, had his coffee, read the paper, gone for a walk by the water. When he came back to the house, Isabelle had set out his suit for the day. He always wore a suit to work. He had twenty of them. All dark. All tailored to his frame, which was tall, solid, but not large. Many of his younger colleagues dressed more casually than he had throughout his career. He might have noticed this, but it didn't bother him. He wasn't that kind of man. He lived too much in his head to be bothered by the habits of others, except for some students.

He stood in front of the mirror, his aftershave still wet on his cheeks as his fingers quickly folded the fabric of his tie into a tight knot at his neck. He folded down his collar and walked into the other room, where Isabelle sat watching TV, one of the morning shows. She turned to him as he walked in.

"Don't forget Jonathan's birthday this evening."

"Of course not."

Jonathan was their grandson.

"We're meeting at The Dahlia Lounge at six. Then going back to Jean and Cindy's house to open presents."

"I'll be there. Will you need a ride?"

"They're picking me up on the way."

Michel nodded his head. He knew today would be busy. They had interviews for the PhD program all day, not to mention the arrival of Jeff Pepper first thing that morning. He was not easily impressed, but this was a big deal. It wasn't every day the world's third richest man arrived to watch his grant dollars at work. Everything about the visit was unusual, planned only the week before. His people had called the department to set up the date. Raj Gupta had almost had a heart attack, first panicking, then growing flustered, then irritable, and finally, self-important; it was a familiar pattern. The grant was in his laboratory. He'd been nothing if not secretive about its progress. Michel clenched his teeth. He never criticized people, and he'd never say it out loud, but he didn't like Raj. He didn't trust him. If he'd had a say, the man would never have stayed in the department as long as he had, but it had never been his decision to make. Michel had just been an assistant professor when the man was hired. He'd been tied up in his own research, his own dreams of discovery and awards. Plus, Raj had been Roger Dibble's pet project. Roger had recruited him specifically, based on the man's transcript, his sparkling research publications, and his single-minded focus. It had been an unusual choice, as Roger had always disdained the very type of scientist Raj had shown every sign of being, even from day one. There was no balance. Like everyone in the department, Raj was married with kids. He was young, 28, 29 at the most when he came to the University over 25 years ago.

From his first day he'd proven himself a first-class asshole. He interrupted people. He talked over them. He changed subjects on a whim. Blatantly ignored specific requests. He had his post-docs write all his papers before he slapped on his corresponding author credit. But most tellingly to Michel, it seemed the man ignored his family. That was the big problem, he was always there. If Michel came in early to prepare for a lecture, Raj would be there, hunched at his desk. When he left at night, Raj would be in his lab, delegating work to his post-docs, all of whom he clearly treated with contempt. These were all signs of a poor researcher. If there was no balance, then there was no time for the mind to recover and think. Einstein had had a family life and a whole slew of mistresses. It was when you were quiet, or in Einstein's case, when you were screwing around, that the mind flourished. When you're always pushing paper and bustling along in pursuit of the awards and the expanding list of publications, that's when you lose sight of what the research is all about - trying to make things *better* for people! Raj didn't care about people, which meant he'd *never* win that Nobel Prize he felt certain was in his future. Michel smirked to himself. How many decades had he stood in the mirror, putting on his tie, musing about Raj? Now Roger was long retired, and Michel was stuck with his friend's pet project, whom both of them, Roger included, had come to despise. Had Raj not been so entirely oblivious to the opinions of others, he would clearly have picked up on the loathing Renoir directed towards him, but as it was, he was clueless. Now there was this Jeff Pepper business to deal with, and Raj would be like the prize peacock, strutting around the department, preening his feathers and looking down his nose at the rest of the department. It would be unbearable.

Truth be told, he couldn't recall what it was that Raj was working on these days. He'd heard the budget names batted back and forth the last few years, but he'd heard so many study names over his time in the field that the details of each had long since faded from his memory. He wasn't alone in this respect. So many studies, so many trials and test groups. They all blended together, one after the other. One stream, one blur of money and announcements. Occasionally this work bred results, but it mostly spawned an incestuous slurry of publications to be cited and recited in paper after paper - " a tale of tedium and drudgery, signifying nothing." It sometimes came as a bit of a surprise when the names they'd tossed around in the labs and throughout the department over the years were suddenly published in the newspapers, ballyhooed as the new magic drug or breakout commodity on Wall Street.

To Michel, the transition from the world of research to the world of production for profit was a leap he'd never gotten used to. To Raj it was the bridge to money and acclaim. Michel had his doubts about Raj's arrangements outside of the department. He'd never been one with an axe to grind, but something in his gut told him there was more to Raj's interests than was reported back in faculty meetings. Sooner or later they'd need to look a little deeper, make sure nothing was percolating below the surface that might cause trouble for the department.

"Michel, I think that's tied."

He stopped. He'd been obsessing, straightening the knot on his tie 'til his fingers had worried it into a virtual noose. Now he pried the fabric apart with his finger nails. His face was red with irritation.

"I was just thinking about my morning."

"I know who you were thinking about darling. I just hope one of you retires before he gives you a heart attack."

Michel laughed. He knew Raj would never retire.

"I think I'm the one who'll have to call it quits if I ever want to get away from that frustration."

"Then retire. Please."

She said it playfully, but he knew she was serious. Isabelle had hated Raj since the day she met him. She felt he was unscrupulous. From time to time she'd even called him evil. Michel had been ready to retire for the last few years, but a part of him was afraid to see what would happen to the department if he left. But he had to go soon. His own research was virtually completed. His labs were closing down. He was more involved with administrative duties than anything else, but his mind wasn't in it. He was ready to travel again, go back to France with Isabelle. Catch up with friends in Europe and back east. By the end of this school year he felt sure he'd be ready to throw in the towel.

"What's on your agenda for the day?" he asked her.

"Birthday shopping. Getting a house-warming gift for Stephen and Kelly."

Stephen was another of their sons. Their kids were all growing up, buying houses and having families. God he felt old.

"That should be nice."

She turned to him slowly.

"I'll miss you."

"I'll miss you too."

He lifted his wallet and car keys from the valet on top of his dresser, put them in his pockets, and walked over to her. He bent down and kissed her.

"I'll see you at dinner tonight."

"See you tonight," she responded.

Isabelle saw a brief flash as sunlight hit the leather on his shoe as he rounded the corner and left the room. Then he was gone. She felt a tug at the corners of her mouth. A sinking feeling tugged at her stomach. She didn't know why. There was no reason to feel this way. It was odd, but there it was, and then she said it, to the silence of the room.

"Be careful."

22

PEPPER

There were three patio sculptures visible from the bed in the master suite, each of a different Roman emperor. He couldn't recall their names. Since he had no alarm clock, no deadlines, no unwanted demands on his time, there was seldom any reason for him to get up at a predetermined hour. Of all the perks that came with wealth, that was probably his favorite. Even so, he hated to let an entire day go by while he slept, so he made a point of rising by ten on most days. He hated alarm clocks. Electric, windup, they all set him on edge. Even the sound of an alarm in a radio ad or TV commercial could send him through the roof. Instead of a clock, he slept with the blinds open, and judged time by the three statues. If he woke and sunlight was on the left side of the first statue's face, it was far too early to be doing anything. If he opened his eyes and saw a glow on the third emperor's right profile, he leapt out of bed, ready to play catch-up, whatever that catching up might entail.

Today he opened his eyes and saw a dim light landing square on top of the second statue's head. Normally, this would be an ungodly early hour for him, what the working folks called 9 a.m., but this was a busy day. He'd scheduled several events that he was looking forward to, and one which he'd been wanting to scratch off his list for quite some time now.

His name was Jeff Pepper. Age: 52. He was five foot eleven inches tall, with a medium sized frame, and a slight paunch from too many nights spent eating well and to excess. His hair was salt and pepper grey - extra salt at the temples. His face was smooth but blotchy. He had terrible teeth. They'd always been bad, but an illness in his early thirties had required serious treatments - chemicals pumped through his body, radiation, test drugs - they'd saved his life, but one or all of them had made his teeth even worse. He never asked his doctors if that was true, it was simply his guess, a self-diagnosis. It was also his opinion that fixing his teeth would erase the only sign that he had almost died. They reminded him that each day he was living on borrowed time. Still, in a year or so he *might* have some work done. When he greeted people at events, or welcomed them aboard his yacht, he knew exactly what they were thinking when they shook his hand and opened their eyes wide, if only for the briefest second, before pumping his arm and returning the smile. They really were terrible teeth. Aside from that, there was nothing extraordinary about his appearance. Someone meeting him on the street might mistake him for a salesman of some kind, or someone who worked with numbers. In a way he did work with numbers, billion dollar figures, all of them his own.

He was loaded. Beyond loaded. His net worth was the stuff of legend. The type of figure that had to be removed when calculating averages for the regions in which he owned property. If the third-richest man in the world lives in a city, figuring the value of each citizen's estate is thrown off by a discrepancy in the tens of billions of dollars. He had done well for himself, very well for a skin-of-the-teeth high school graduate with only two weeks of college education. His wealth came from a childhood hobby – computers. He and his friend had written some code, designed some software, and started up a business. As it so happened, they did this at just the right time, as people were starting to bring some new tools into their homes, including the personal computer. Their products were just what was needed, and since they'd struck at such an opportune moment, using just the right plan, they'd managed to corner the market on 97 percent of the computers in the world. That meant Jeff's pockets had been well lined since his 22nd birthday. By 31 he had almost died, but he didn't. He underwent the medical treatments, lived in the compound he'd bought for his family in eastern Seattle, and read - classics, contemporary volumes, new age, Zen, true crime, mystery, the whole caboodle. Then, once he'd gotten better, he started buying stuff, and starting stuff, and doing the things he'd always dreamed of. In the last 20 odd years he'd tried his best to spend all his money, but it just kept pouring in, despite the fact that he never went back to work for the company he had co-founded. What was the point?

Now he sat in his bed. The silk pajama top was cool on his chest, just the right temperature. The air in the room moved ever so gently, again, just to his specifications. He spun his legs over the edge of the bed, paused to take a deep breath, then stood up and walked across the room to an enormous television set. He turned it to the 24-hour business news channel, glanced down at the ticker tape stock updates running along the bottom of the screen, then cranked up the volume and walked into the closet suite, where row after row of warm, low lighting glowed down on the racks of suits and shoes. The lights brightened as he entered the room, a ring of light following him down the aisle as he picked out his clothes for the day. He heard the sound of Will's shoes padding across the carpet in the main room. In olden times, folks would have called Will his butler, his right hand man, the Jeeves to his Wooster. 'Course, Will was just the front line for an extensive support staff. He knew how things worked behind the scenes. Yes, Jeff could lounge in bed all day, deciding when to get up on a whim, what his routine would be, but at the same time, there was a small army of people always on hand, watching, waiting to see when he would need what, and for exactly how long. His staff, the full staff, not just the 24 hour people, had probably been at the compound for two hours now. His cook, Theresa, would have had breakfast ready for each of them as they showed up on site and were briefed for the day. The staff needed to know of any work being done on the property, any guests staying at the compound, and any special events taking place that day or later in the week. Everyone ate breakfast during the meeting. Then, after they left, Theresa would prepare Jeff's meal, usually the same menu she prepared for the workers, which she'd then put on standby, ready for delivery the moment she got the word from upstairs.

On certain occasions, Jeff enjoyed getting up early, without warning, and slipping into the line to eat with the crowd. A few times he'd actually taken them by surprise, but now he thought they were looking for him, and much as he enjoyed eating with them, he didn't want them to get out of practice, especially if he had any lady friends over. His female companions seemed to love the morning service just the way it was.

Nevertheless, Jeff knew that the moment someone in the hall had heard his TV switch on, a series of events had been set in motion downstairs. Word went from person to person. A call was no doubt made to his personal assistants from the foundation to let them know he was on the move. Theresa would have put the finishing touches on his breakfast, set it on a serving platter, and whisked it out the kitchen door, where someone placed the day's newspapers next to the covered dish as it passed through the main hallway. The tray went up the stairs, down another hallway, and was finally placed in the hands of William, who brought it inside, arranged the meal on the nightstand beside Jeff's bed, and went about tidying the room and silently correcting Jeff's mistakes.

"Sir, I have your breakfast ready," William called assertively from the main room.

"I'll be there in one minute, Will. What do we have today?"

"Theresa went with a Mexican theme for the day. Quite good actually, but a bit on the spicy side. Huevos rancheros."

"Huevos rancheros, eh? Do I have practice today?"

"Yes. Mr. Morita is setting up now. He should be ready for you in an hour."

Mr. Morita was his trainer. Jeff been studying one form of martial arts or another for the last 15 years. He didn't know that he was any good, but it was fun; it appealed to the nerdy computer programmer in him, he guessed. Jeff grabbed a shirt and tie off one of the shelves and headed towards the smell of food.

"If I'm gonna be kicking and jumping around, I better start digesting this spicy breakfast."

Jeff emerged from the closet with the clothes, which he tossed on an armchair to the side of the bathroom door, and sat down to eat. Will walked over to the chair and straightened the suit. He glanced at the shirt and tie and picked them up. They didn't match. He turned to Jeff, who was taking a massive bite.

"Phew," Jeff fanned his mouth. "These *are* spicy."

"Ms. Parker and Mr. Drake have also been phoned."

Jeff nodded. Those were his main people from the foundation, Nina and David, the ones who channeled all the information to him about, well, everything - his investments, his charity, his work, what needed his attention, what didn't. He thought of them as not just his eyes and ears, but his arms and his legs. They kept his circus going.

"Great. Anything else I should know about?"

"I believe that's everything," Will replied as he slipped into the closet, quickly selected a better shirt and tie, and picked up a different pair of shoes.

"Did Nina say anything about the University?"

"Yes, they're expecting you around noon."

Jeff looked at the clock at the bottom corner of the TV: 9:06. He glanced at the statues outside the window. They never failed him.

"Great, they're probably gonna wanna eat lunch over there. I better take it easy on this."

Will walked back into the room, slipping the newly selected accessories beside the suit, unnoticed.

Jeff turned back to the TV. He thought someone onscreen

had said his name, but nothing they were discussing seemed to relate to him. No logos were on the screen for one of his companies. He must have imagined it. Megalomania was setting in. He thought everything was about him. Well, probably not, they probably had dropped his name. If they didn't mention the other guy in the company a few times an hour, then they mentioned him, the weird one, the guy who'd left, but still made all the money. They were the winners of the greatest widget award. Hell, their software was probably running every graphic he was seeing on screen. Jesus, was he ever bored with programming.

He took another forkful of eggs, chewing slowly as he thought things over. Today. Today, he was going to the University to check on one of his grants that had been nagging at him. He had tons of grants out there, tons of research and education and public service money circulating, probably more than he even knew, but he tried to keep some tabs on them whenever they came to mind. The people at the foundation handled all of it for him, but as Oprah once said, no matter how rich you are, you've gotta sign your own checks. Otherwise, you ended up like Elvis, or Howard Hughes, or Britney. No, he couldn't lump himself in with Britney yet. But the point was, you stop signing the checks and people get control of your money, they insulate you, they let you become "eccentric," then fully insane, then they grab the rubber stamp with your signature, and sell themselves the farm. He swallowed his eggs and looked over at Will.

Will wouldn't steal my farm, he thought to himself as he watched the guy inspecting his suit, pulling at a piece of thread that didn't meet his approval. Will was his Jeeves all right; all he cared about was that Jeff didn't walk out of the house looking like anything less than a dapper billionaire. Jeff pulled out his own outfits each morning, but he knew Will shuffled them around each day. For all he knew, Will was in on it too, like most wealthy folks, this was one of his little amusements.

So he was going to the University because something was bothering him. A red flag of sorts had popped up. He had tons of funding out there, but he also had his pet projects, things he got excited about, or started up, then usually lost interest in, but kept funding. It was one of those projects that he was going to check on. He was a sci-fi nut, so lots of his personal projects came from watching old movies and TV shows. Occasionally something newer would pique his interest. In 1995 he'd seen that Dustin Hoffman movie *Outbreak,* which had given him an idea. That was back when the Ebola virus was the worry of choice. There'd been books, documentaries, two competing movie projects, all about that issue. How he'd ended up seeing the Hoffman movie he couldn't recall, must have been on the plane, or maybe he'd produced it. Well, that had given him an idea, he wanted to fund research to find a way to treat this sort of virus outbreak. The movie opened on a village in trouble, with two apparent researchers investigating the problem, only to leave and call in an air strike that drops a hydrogen bomb on the site. Not exactly a cure, but it had gotten Jeff thinking. What if someone could come up with something that *could* treat those people? A formulation of *something* that could be dropped from a plane onto an infected village and instantly treat every man, woman, and child on the ground. He didn't know how they'd do it, but he must have seen something like it on *Star Trek* or somewhere. He'd talked to Nina about it, who took the idea away with her, wrote up a proposal, ran it past him again, and then sent it out.

That was 12 years ago. Eventually they'd gone with someone at the University in Seattle, a world renowned guy who seemed like a dream choice for the project, and that had been that. From time to time Jeff had heard updates on the progress, or received a copy of an article that had been published in one of the journals. Then it had all faded from his thoughts, until about six months ago that is, when he'd suddenly remembered the whole idea. He'd probably caught a rerun of *Outbreak* on Spike TV after a James Bond marathon and asked Nina to get him everything she could find on that "Ebola bomb cure thing" as he put it. So she'd done some checking and brought him a big binder full of stuff, but when he read over everything, it didn't add up. They'd been funding it for a dozen years, and yet, aside from a few early findings and a handful of studies, no publications had been coming out of the lab that in any way related to *cures*. The foundation had kept sending the checks, and the researcher, some Raj guy, had kept cashing them, but nothing he published to meet the grant requirements seemed to have anything to do with cures. Everything was about ways to propel whatever substance he'd devised into as wide an area as possible. Jeff was no scientist, but everything he was reading seemed to be about "the bomb" part of the idea, with nothing about what exactly would be scattered through the air to stop the infections.

A murmur in his gut told him something was fishy.

He almost always went with his gut. It had treated him well

31

over the years, told him when to start his company, when to leave, when he had cancer, and when something wasn't right. At the moment, his gut was hurting him, and it wasn't from the huevos rancheros. He wanted to meet with this researcher face to face, get a tour of the labs, bring along some experts from the foundation and see what they thought was going on. Nina had set up the appointment the week before. He had no doubt the scene at the University was chaos and confusion as they prepared for his arrival. Good. If nothing else, it would be interesting.

He finished the eggs and slid the plate to the edge of the nightstand. He'd had too many. Hopefully Mr. Morita would go easy on him today, but probably not. Will had set up his suit for after practice, and was just coming in with Jeff's workout clothes. Jeff stood up, took the white pants and top, and walked into the bathroom. He was done thinking about the grant inspection for the time being. Now he was trying to remember the moves Morita had taught him last week. He motioned with his hands absentmindedly, trying to remember that particular defense. Hopefully the old guy wouldn't pull it on him first thing. Ah who was he kidding? Morita always pulled that stuff on him. Jeff didn't mind, and Morita always said to him, "You want to be fat, dimheaded billionaire, or do you want to keep sharp?"

Sharp, sensei. Sharp.

Jeff closed the bathroom door and changed into his workout clothes.

"TIM"

His name wasn't Tim, not even close, but for some reason people always thought that it was. He just looked familiar to them, and the same name always came to mind: Tim. So that was the name he went by here. His friends told him he looked more American than the rest of them, whatever that meant; he took it as an insult, but he had to admit there was something different about him. He had no trouble blending in with society, a face that disappeared in the crowd. No threatening gestures. No severe angle to his brow. Nothing to make people suspicious, or wary, or alert.

He was a man of average qualities. Average looks. Average height, around five foot ten. Average weight. Average build. He had short brown hair and a set of matching eyes. Nothing about him was made to stand out. But still, when he looked in the mirror, he caught glimpses of traits he knew he had to work on. A glint in the eye. A set to his mouth. Both of which he feared would give him away, flashes of pride and anger.

So why was he in America? It was the last place he wanted to be. He didn't hate Americans. He didn't hate the country.

It just wasn't his. He wanted to be home, with his family, but he'd been sent away on a mission, and so he had gone. His own country was forever at risk, always in danger of being taken from its people. That was the way things were, the way they'd always been, but it didn't have to stay that way, not forever.

Growing up, when two kids on a playground get into a tussle and one knocks the other down, common wisdom is to fight back, stand your ground, shove the kid and he'll learn his lesson. When Tim was a boy and the bully had come for him, he didn't shove him back. No, Tim had taken a pocketknife and stabbed it between his classmate's ribs, collapsing his lung and bubbling blood to his lips. The boy had left Tim alone after that. He had to; he'd ended up in the hospital. Tim on the other hand had wound up in a special school, one specially designed to reform young boys who stabbed their comrades with pocket knives. But the school didn't reform him, it couldn't. He hadn't stabbed an equal, he'd stabbed a bully, someone lesser than himself. An infidel. Even then, he knew the only way to make your point, to make it *last*, was to strike first, and if not first, then to strike hardest. It someone hurt one of yours, you killed two of theirs. If they used clubs and stones, you used fire.

That was what he was doing today, arming his people with fire.

They'd been preparing for this day for years. Finding their targets, making their plans. They knew what they needed, they'd learned where to find it, and they set about the scheme methodically. There were issues of money, all the variables of living in one country with the intent of gaining weapons for another. For the last year they'd known exactly what they wanted and where to find it.

He stood before the mirror in the front hall of the home he'd lived in for the past two years. This was one of several places they had set up during their time in the U.S.. It was a nice home. He'd actually grown fond of it. He really didn't mind Americans. He didn't want to hurt them, but all the same, he wasn't one of them. He liked the place he had been staying, but it could never be home. He knew the facts, and they were hard ones. Sometimes some sacrifices must be made for the greater good. Some of those sacrifices would come today. He crouched down for a moment, unzipping a dark green duffel bag, once more going through its contents, methodically checking each item, each piece of equipment. His movements were mechanical, swift and precise, as they would have to be for the rest of the day. He couldn't think. Couldn't let emotions come into play, not for what he had to do. Half his men were outside. The rest of them were on their way. They'd descend on the building at the predetermined time. Everything was set. There was no stopping it. No turning back.

He zipped up the bag, heaved its weight over his shoulder, and walked out the door.

BEHIND CLOSED DOORS

Fucking in broom closets was hot as hell. And it only grew hotter as time went on.

Nick and Morgan had made that discovery early on.

When they first made the leap from flirtation to physical relationship, they'd tried to keep it out of the office. Nick knew there were rules regarding affairs between faculty and students. He'd never heard anything about relationships between staff and students, and doubted any guidelines were in place, but still, he didn't want to run the risk of learning the hard way. Plus, his boss was a world-class, bureaucratic tight ass (ironic considering her penchant for carbs - donuts, scones, family-sized fiddle faddle - which had left her physical ass a real estate challenger second only to the British Empire at its global peak) so he'd seen no sense in taking chances.

For the first few months they'd gone to Morgan's apartment each afternoon. Then she'd started teasing him. He'd be sitting at his desk, reading some *God awful* paper about *God knows what*, when she'd walk by his cubicle, stop for a moment, then duck in and kiss him on the neck, then on the mouth. By the time her seduction techniques had advanced to running just the tip of her tongue up to his earlobe as she slipped her hand down to his crotch and gave him a gentle squeeze, Nick had had enough of the self-restraint business. He sat frozen, shocked, but tingling. Morgan left the cubicle, walked down the hallway, and out of the office. Nick followed close behind. They went looking for a place to fuck, and found one in the corner of an all-but-forgotten wing of the psychology department. To anyone walking down the unlit hall, the doorway looked like the entrance to a closed-up bathroom, but when you slipped around the corner and down the short hallway, you were met by a door with no sign. They'd pushed on that door slowly, not knowing if they'd find someone on the other side, but fortunately, all they'd uncovered was an empty room, about six feet square, containing two brooms and an old desk chair. A soft desk chair.

Morgan unzipped the front of Nick's jeans as soon as he closed the door, slipping her hand inside and rubbing him as she unbuttoned her shirt. It was all Nick could do to get the door locked before falling back into the chair. She pulled off his pants, then stood up, slipped off her panties, and walked over to him. He leaned forward, cupping her breasts and slowly twirling his tongue around one nipple as she climbed onto the chair, straddled him with her legs, and lowered herself down over him.

That was how they'd done it in the closet that first time, and that was how they were doing it now. He knew they were pushing their luck. By this point, if someone in the office didn't know what they were doing, then they must have at least had their suspicions. Today of all days they couldn't afford to be slipping out for 20 to 30 minutes at a time for sexcapades around the health sciences complex. Someone would be needing *something* from one them, and when they couldn't find Nick at his desk, or Morgan at the front table, they'd starting putting one and one together. The thing was, he didn't care. He wrapped his arms under her and pulled Morgan tighter against him as she ground her body into him. He kissed her breasts and ran his tongue up her neck, losing himself in her blond hair and the sounds of her moaning.

They'd get back to the office soon enough. For now there were better things to do.

***

He'd gotten off the bus earlier than usual that day. There had still been that damp, cool feeling of morning in the air as he walked into the building. The front lobby was filled with the usual cast of characters: the homeless guy who cooked all of his meals in the microwave near the vending machines; the group of lab technicians, all in their fifties, with scraggly beards and flannel shirts, who sat at the table each morning, drinking coffee, reading the paper, and laughing away - eternal graduate students. Then there were the real students, studying their papers, highlighting pages in their books, or talking on their cell phones before their morning classes. Nick stumbled past all of this, half asleep, but mentally restless. He was thinking about the writing he'd done that morning. It had been going slowly lately. He was working on a novel, but fighting his own impatience to be done. He wondered if he should try the same story as a screenplay. No. He had to be patient. Then his mind went to Morgan, and he tried to force himself to think about work.

He walked through the department door to find the offices abuzz with activity. The administrative staff was copying handouts and making last-minute adjustments to the schedule. This was the big day. Jeff Pepper would be here around lunchtime to go through the facility and talk to Raj.

Raj.

Fucking cock.

Nick hated the man. He'd probably be in good and early today, with his pompous little rooster walk and his cracking ankle. That's how he always knew when that asshole was walking by; he could hear his goddamn ankle cracking with each and every step.

Nick rounded the corner and started down the main hallway, bumping into Sandy, the main administrator, the one with the sizable posterior real estate holdings.

"Good morning," he said reluctantly.

"Oh, it's crazy. It's crazy. Happy *MONDAY!*"

"Big day…"

"To say the least. We're barely gonna make it. I don't know what I'm gonna do. Raj hasn't even shown up yet and I just-"

Nick mentally tuned her out as she disappeared into the copy room. He kept on walking, lest she come back out and undergo her first mood swing of the day. Sandy was always in a tizzy about something, but he knew that was the way she liked it. Having someone like Jeff Pepper coming in was the ultimate excuse for panic and anxiety. She'd get everything done in plenty of time. Hell, it was probably already done. She was not a busy woman, just an excitable, self-important bureaucracy fetishist.

He got to his cubicle, turned on the fluorescent desk lights, and switched on the computer. He was getting a bit more excited about Jeff Pepper's visit too. He wasn't one for computers or programming, or even for business really, but something about that guy was fascinating. He had companies for everything. After he co-founded the software place he'd gotten sick, really sick, then he'd recovered and started founding all sorts of funky places. Museums, film companies, construction companies, research labs. Nick had tried getting jobs at a few of them when he first got out of school, but he was never able to get his resume through the logistical hoops set up by all of Pepper's foundations. Maybe it was just as well; cool as all they seemed, he'd heard they weren't the greatest places to work. Course, this certainly wasn't the best place to work either. There was nothing creative about his job, which had been fine at first, but now it was starting to wear on him. That was no doubt one reason his daytime trysts with Morgan were becoming more and more frequent. Well, that and the fact that he couldn't stop thinking about the girl, which worried him. He'd have to resolve things with Kendra soon. That was over, he was sure of it. She must have met someone else, and the truth was, he didn't care all that much. He needed to talk to Morgan too. He didn't want to scare her off, but she *was* just a sophomore in college, after all. Boy, life was a pain in the ass.

Speaking of pains in one's ass, that was when he heard the dreaded cracking sound strutting down the hall toward him. Fucking Raj. All in all, the job shouldn't have been that bad. He

Mike Attebery

didn't know what the hell he was editing, and the field could not have interested him any less. Yeah, drugs went through peoples bodies, and they were absorbed and processed in all sorts of fascinating and mind-blowing ways, but Nick didn't give a shit. He wasn't a scientist. Let someone else spend his life shriveling up under fluorescent lights, recording data, and writing boring, *boooring* research papers to report their findings, just don't let that person be him. So he went to work, and he edited the papers, which was like trying to put grammar in a page of Chinese text, it was all foreign to him. A few of the professors were nice enough. They appreciated his work. At Christmas they'd given him Starbucks gift cards.

Then there was Raj. Raj was the department prima donna, the type of academic researcher Nick was starting to learn existed in every department at the university. One of the secretaries had described Raj perfectly during Nick's first week on the job. Raj was the egomaniacal rooster in the department hen house. He sat in his office, appearing terribly, terribly busy and important, he assigned papers and studies, he made phone calls, went to meetings, and he wandered around telling people what he wanted them to do, but all in all, he himself did nothing. In the year that Nick had worked in the department, about 85 percent of his work had come from Raj. Raj had papers to submit. Raj had publisher proofs to correct. Raj had monumentally important reports to write, articles to cowrite. It was that whole cowriting bit that really pissed Nick off. The guy didn't write a thing! He just had his post-docs and collaborators put together dozen upon dozens of drafts, then he'd cherry pick the bits he liked and slap his name on the front of them. An exploiting, plagiarizing fraud. He used people. Nick realized this was how the man did everything. His researchers were all from countries like India, China, and Japan. Their visas all came through Raj's office, he chose whom he wanted, then the college filed the forms, so that once these researchers were there, working as post-docs for Raj, they were basically indentured servants, subject to the whims and abuses of Raj Gupta, researcher extraordinaire. Nick's dislike for the man was growing worrisome. He hated the way the guy talked down to him in his singsong voice. He hated the way his researchers scampered in and out of the guy's office, bobbing their heads submissively, all but tripping over themselves as they attempted to keep their great leader happy. The guy was beneath contempt, but Nick was generous and heaped him with mountains of gooey disdain. The one thing that bothered Nick the most about Raj, and the thing that warned him that Raj was coming while simultaneously tensing up every muscle in his back, was the sound of Raj's goddamn cracking ankle. He couldn't understand it. The guy worked in a medical research complex, *attached to a hospital.* He spent his days surrounded by reports on medical findings and ways to keep the human body running smoothly, and yet, as he strutted around the hallways, head held high, his little moustache squished against his nose by his pursed upper lip, his ankle made a sharp cracking noise with each step. It was the most annoying sound Nick had ever heard. It drove him up the walls. It made him long for Morgan to come in, so they could sneak away, and fool around, and be free of that *sound* and everything it stood for. Course, today he couldn't afford to mess around. Raj would be in fine form. He had important visitors coming and there was no time to waste.

43

And now, here he was, and with him, that joyful *crack crack crack* of his grinding, scraping, popping bones.

Raj strutted past the entrance to Nick's cube.

Crack crack.

If Raj turned and said hello, it meant he had work to dump on Nick. Raj *never* said hello unless he wanted something. Nick stared at his screen, avoiding eye contact as he heard the little rooster digging through his pockets, looking for his keys.

Jingle. Jingle jingle.

Nick held his breath as a key slipped into a lock, and the door to Raj's offices opened with a wheezing squeak. Then... then...

Crack, crack, crack, crack...

Raj walked into his office. Nick could already hear him punching his code into the phone to listen to his messages over the speaker phone (as *all* horribly busy men must do). Everyone must know who was trying to reach Raj, and why, and how often they called. The worst was the sound of Raj calling these people back, often while post-docs or graduate students were in the room.

The messages played, "Hello Dr. Gupta, this is Nina Parker from Mr. Pepper's office calling. Just a reminder that we'll be arriving this afternoon around twelve. Please have everything ready for Mr. Pepper's arrival; he doesn't like to be kept waiting. Oh, and please don't force him to ask questions during the the visit. All information should be shared in a forthcoming manner. I believe you know what that means. Oh, and Dr. Gupta? He can tell when people aren't telling him everything, trust me."

Nick's ears perked up. The messages from the Pepper Foundation had grown blunt over the last several weeks. That wasn't a good thing for Raj, but Nick found it extremely interesting. It sounded like Pepper was getting suspicious about Raj's work. Nick had been suspicious about his work from the get-go. He had edited a few of the papers that came out of the lab, and though he understood little of what was being discussed, he was able to extrapolate *some* information about the program, but it was sketchy. As best he could tell, the money from the Pepper Foundation was funding a project aimed at halting the spread of an airborne virus and quickly reversing its incubation in subjects. Early on, there had been a few papers examining the effects of the virus in several of the monkeys in the primate center. Research papers never reported failures; those were brushed under the rug, but these reports did seem to show promising advancement toward the goal.

Yet for the last six or seven months Nick hadn't seen anything from the lab. He did edit one early draft of a paper discussing the best manner in which to disperse substances into the air once a vaccine formulation had been finalized, but even that had been a strange manuscript. Nick felt it would have been better suited to an entirely different department, maybe something in applied physics or the engineering school. Either way, that had been the last paper to come out of Gupta's lab in months. Either the research was going badly, or it had veered off target. Maybe Pepper was getting the same impression.

Jeff Pepper.

In the back of his mind, Nick couldn't help but think that making contact with the man was as good a way as any (and better than most) to get his work seen by people who mattered, maybe even get it produced by one of the Pepper Foundation's publishing and entertainment branches. If the circumstances had been any different, if the visit weren't so riddled with doubt and apprehension, Nick might even have brought something in with him, maybe just a short story. But the thing was, Nick had an inkling of why the guy was coming in. It was just a stab in his gut, but he'd felt it for a while now. Maybe it was fear, or dread, but Nick's instincts told him he knew something he wasn't meant to. He still didn't know if Raj had seen him that day.

Right after Christmas, Nick had been trying to track Raj down in the labs to get an author release signed for one of the research journals. It had been one of those rare days when Nick was looking for Raj, rather than trying to avoid the man at all costs. Finally, when the journal had emailed for a third time, saying that they really, absolutely, *without delay*, needed the paperwork signed *now,* Nick had gone looking for the little man. When he couldn't find him in any of the Health Science Building labs, he'd headed down to the Primate Center, which was located several stories below the building's western wing. Nick was surprised his identification badge had gotten him all the way down to the heart of the center. No one had given him more than a passing glance as he walked down corridor after corridor, asking the whereabouts of the Gupta lab. Finally, a small Asian woman rushed past him, and Nick had to all but clothesline her with his arm to get her to stop.

"Excuse me, can you tell me where to find the Gupta laboratory?"

"Which one?" she asked sharply.

"The Pepper Foundation facility?" Nick guessed.

She lifted her arm and pointed to the end of the hall. "There."

Then she was gone, once again shuffling down the corridor.

That was when Nick saw it. A quick, split-second snapshot, the briefest flash before his eyes, but one that burned itself into his mind. He'd rounded the corner, head down, looking over the paperwork, when his gaze turned upwards, towards a small viewing portal in one of the walls. That's where he'd seen it, just for a millisecond, the pleading gaze of a monkey's eyes, sharp and terrified, staring through the glass at him. The air was filling with a sort of mist. He could hear a hissing sound in the background, then…

Phoom!

The face and eyes were gone.

Nick turned in horror, stumbling to the side as he covered his eyes, but the image was stuck there, every gory detail. The animal had disintegrated, its insides turned out. Every blood vessel, every opening on its face -- eyes, mouth, nose -- in an instant, they had sprayed a puff of red, curdled inward, then torn apart in a bloody cloud of fluids and pulpy tissue.

That wasn't research going on in those labs. That was testing.

That's when Nick turned and ran to the elevators. He rode them back to the Department of Immunology's main floor, sat down at his desk, and held his head in his hands. Just as he was doing now, all these months later.

The memory had briefly silenced the office around him. Then the squeak of a desk chair, and the "pop" of Raj's ankle.

Nick turned in his chair, just as the *"great scientist"* peered around the corner of the cubicle wall.

"Uhhhhh…." Nick heard the thick spit sputtering in the back of Raj's throat as he stuttered around for the right word. "Nick. I'm going to have some paperwork for you to go over later, okay?"

Nick nodded his head.

Raj held his gaze for a moment. "I'll drop that off for you later, all right?"

"Okay." Nick responded.

"Just a few things, you know?"

Jesus, Nick thought through a forced smile, I fucking know already! Why did this guy always repeat rhetorical questions long after he'd gotten a clear response?

Then Morgan walked by. Quickly and silently. Nick caught her eyes as she glanced over Raj's shoulder. He knew the look well. She wanted to sneak off to the storage room.

Raj continued nodding his head and blathering away, but Nick was no longer listening. At last the annoying little man shuffled off and Nick rose from his chair, walked past Morgan's desk in the workroom, and headed upstairs. Morgan waited an agonizing minute, then followed after him.

Moments later they were upstairs in the dark, door locked, clothes stripped away, hearts ready to explode.

***

Jeff looked down at the approaching helicopter pad on the roof of the University Hospital. He glanced at his watch

- 11:52. Perfect timing. Not too early and definitely not late. A brisk walk through the corridors, his people at his sides, and they'd be arriving for their meeting right on time. He could be scatterbrained at times, but whether or not people waited for important people was beside the point for him; in his mind, important people didn't leave others waiting, 'cause they didn't have time to waste.

The rotor blades whipperwooled overhead as the copter came in for a landing, its skids gently setting down on the concrete. Jeff secretly loved the bustle of such arrivals. He was notorious for his secretive activities and his private personality -- when people talked of his old company, he was inevitably referred to as the "phantom co-founder" or the "accidental gazillionaire" -- but that didn't bother him. He preferred to remain less well known than his old high school friend, who'd stuck with the company and wound up assuming the position of world's wealthiest man. For Jeff, it was more fun to have the perks, the wealth, the fame, but go through life with fewer ruffled feathers, so that when someone *did* recognize him, he could still feign cluelessness but savor the kick of recognition.

A young guy, probably a hospital PR rep, walked up to the copter, accompanied by a landing attendant. They held the cabin doors open as Jeff, Nina, and David disembarked. The PR guy was shouting something at them, but Jeff neither heard nor paid attention to what he was saying. They followed their greeters across the roof toward an open doorway where another guy, a college age kid, was waiting anxiously. This guy clearly knew who Jeff was. He was probably a business major, working at the hospital on a co-op or something. He wore an ill-fitted suit, his hair, tie, and shoes all ever so slightly mismatched, not quite tailored to his posture, but he was on the right track. The kid nodded to him with a smile and Jeff nodded back. The noise from the copter was deafening, but Jeff could just make out the kid's bellowed "Pleasure to meet you!" as he put out his hand, which Jeff reached out and shook. He patted the kid on the shoulder as the group ducked into the building. Then they were off, racing down corridors, Italian leather shoes clapping on linoleum hospital floors. The PR guy chattered away about their schedule and what an honor it was to meet him. Jeff just thought about the kid's expression when he'd shaken his hand. That was the look of excitement. These other people, the hospital reps, they were just bootlicking toadies. Jeff didn't want their tongues smearing his shiny shoes.

***

The guy at the front gate didn't even blink. He didn't nod. Didn't hold his gaze on them. Nothing. He just took Tim's pass, glanced from the picture on the card to the man behind the wheel of the black van, and pushed a button to raise the gate. Tim pulled the van forward and glanced at his companion in the passenger seat, who nodded at him once. Then he continued down the back driveway behind the hospital, looking into his rear view mirror to see if the second group would make it through the security gate with as little notice as he had. He could see the second van coming down the back road to the gate, past the construction site where crews were busy working on the new addition to the hospital. A huge crane towered over the site, its hook and pulley system hoisting materials from the ground and up a dozen stories overhead. Tim's gaze flashed from a rising beam of metal at the end of the crane's cable, back down to the van below, where an arm was reaching out to hand the guard another pass, just like his own. Then the arm pulled back into the cab as the gate opened and the van drove through.

They were in.

It had taken them the better part of two years to get everything in place, from assembling his team in the U.S., to setting up their bank accounts, living arrangements, and jobs. Whenever possible, they'd found ways to get themselves jobs at the university, ones that got them as close as possible to the center of the organization's operations. Most of them worked as janitors. One had even gotten a position in the campus safety department, which had proved immeasurably helpful in forging security clearances for the members of the team that had taken work outside of the university.

Why were they in the United States?

What was their intention?

They weren't terrorists. Not in any traditional sense. Maybe according to Western culture they were, but that was a world whose opinions they did not value. They weren't here to hurt the Americans. They weren't trying to murder or control the people they encountered while carrying out their mission; those people were not the ultimate target. If they got in the way, that might change, Tim knew that neither he nor his men would hesitate to kill or use anyone they encountered in order to further their progress. He had no doubt there would be casualties today, but their goal was not to instill fear; their goal was to find weapons,

weapons no one had ever seen, weapons for which there was no defense. Once they had what they'd come looking for, they would take them to the places where they could best aid in advancing their cause. That was where the real terror would come in, but that was far from here. Still, just because they weren't after Americans, that didn't mean they didn't have their problems with them. Several of his men would have been more than happy to twist their plans back on the people of the country where they had been operating for the last few years. Others found themselves drawn into the culture more than they could ever have thought possible, and those were the ones that might have problems carrying out today's task. Their mission in and of itself was simple, at least on paper: They were here to pick up a weapon. They had found exactly what they'd been looking for and more. If dropping the bomb on Hiroshima had sent a shockwave through the world, stopping the war in its tracks and simultaneously destroying not only the people of the city, but every square inch of land and civilization, then *this* weapon would have that same effect, while keeping the infrastructure and the physical world intact.

As they approached the southeast corner of the building, the road swooped downwards and the van slipped into the darkness of an underground parking facility. Like everything in the mission, their parking arrangements had been carefully mapped out. Tim drove down one level, circled the van around the back corner of the garage, and backed into a spot tucked between two massive concrete support columns. A moment later, the second van approached and backed in beside them. Tim shut down the van's engine and got out of the cab.

"Did you have any problems?" he asked.

The other driver shook his head.

"Then it's time to get started."

The side doors of both vans slid open and a half dozen people slipped out of each vehicle. Their eyes were set, cold and determined, as they filed out into the darkness. There were 14 men total, including Tim. They were all ready, they were all armed, and they were all dressed in Seattle Fire Department gear.

"Check your equipment."

Tim heard the solid, cold sounds of well oiled metal clicking and engaging as his men loaded their firearms and slipped them inside their coats. They stood waiting for his order to move out.

Tim hesitated. Once they began, there was no turning back. He took one deep breath to center himself.

"Let's go."

***

Renoir was running late. Not an uncommon occurrence, but one that irked him terribly. His shoes made little slapping noises as he rushed down the hall of the Health Sciences Building and rounded the corner into the department's entrance. Two of the graduate students were sitting at the front table. Both were long-time students, the variety that never seem to wrap up their studies and actually move out into the working world. Renoir smirked; if they kept this up they'd be on the faculty soon! He didn't know their names. Binky and Dooseldorf sounded good enough to him. Binky was a big, fat guy. Even now, he was sitting at the table, munching on a cinnamon bun as he talked to Dooseldorf, who looked up from the paper as he saw Renoir walking in.

"Good morning Dr. Renoir."

Renoir nodded and walked past them. The receptionist was sitting at the front counter, talking on the phone. He turned right and saw Sandy's office. The door was open, but the manic woman was nowhere in sight.

The rest of the place was quiet. A few of the faculty's office doors were open, but he would have expected more, considering the type of people they were expecting. He had a paper to discuss with the latest editor, a young guy named Mike or Nick or something. He could never remember it. They'd had no so many editors over the years, owing to drama with Sandy or their pure irritation at Raj, that he had long ago stopped getting to know them. Most of the time he just edited his papers himself. Nevertheless, he ducked into the guy's cubicle to ask him a question, but found only an empty chair. The computer was on, though, which meant only one thing. He was off with that student assistant again. That had been going on for months. He hadn't said anything, since a part of him admired how very French it all was. What was the point at working at a college if you couldn't get away with the important stuff. He and Isabelle had been the same way when they'd met during his post-doctoral work.

Renoir glanced into Raj's office. He wasn't there either. Thank God. He'd have a few moments of peace to sit down at his desk, flip through his paper, and gather his energy for the day. He had a feeling he was going to need it.

***

"So what's the plan?" Nina asked.

"What do you mean 'what's the plan?'" David fired back.

They were still marching down the corridor behind the hospital PR guy.

Jeff said nothing. His mouth was held tightly closed as they careened through the building. Students bustled past him. This was bringing back memories from years ago, high school, when he and his best friend had snuck into this same campus to play with the college's computers. They had no idea what they were doing at the time, but now he knew they'd been laying the groundwork that had made their fortunes. Sometimes that bothered him. It felt like he'd had a part in one *big* thing, the creation that had made him his money and set him off from the rest of everything. His other projects were never that successful, but the funny thing was, he was so fucking rich, he couldn't seem to spend the money fast enough. He'd lose several billion dollars, only to find that interest, investments, and shares in the original goose, the one that laid his golden eggs, had once again gone up in value. Weird how things worked out.

"I just don't think this guy is producing." Nina was saying. "And I know Jeff feels the same way."

"About..?" Jeff asked.

David and Nina looked at him with darting, confused eyes.

"About Dr. Gupta not producing," Nina replied.

Jeff gathered his thoughts. Time to stop daydreaming.

Whether he made the money back after he lost it, that was beside the point. He hated losing money, but more than that, he hated being fucked with. This guy Raj Gupta was fucking with him. Jeff stopped walking. Nina and David took another couple of steps, turned around, and walked back to him. The PR guy, who was about ten feet in front of them, also stopped and stood in the middle of the hallway, looking back, wondering if he should walk back to them. David shot him a glance that said, *Mind your business.* Jeff took a step back into a recessed doorway.

"I think this fucker is producing, but I don't think he's producing what we *asked* for. We probably don't even want to know what the fuck he's been doing with the money."

Nina looked at him. Her eyes were two cold gray marbles.

Jeff continued, "I just want to come in, confirm my suspicions, then get out of our arrangement with him. I feel like we're funding a weapons maker."

"Are we?" David asked. "How much do we know?"

Nina held her gaze on Jeff as she answered, "Enough."

"And what do we do once we pull the rug out from under him? Run off with his work?"

"No," Jeff responded, "We call Ransom at the FBI."

***

The little boy was looking at them, but Tim felt nothing. That's what he told himself.

His team's scouts had entered the building through the maintenance stairwells. Their goal was to take in the general situation before they started the big show. Once the first 10 of them had made it past the security counters, they fanned out and began weaving their way through the corridors and back halls of the hospital's research facilities. Their weapons were all hidden away under their fire department uniforms.

Tim walked out of the stairwell and into the main hall. Two of the men directly below him on the chain of command, Guy and Myer, were walking on either side of him. Their expressions were set in stone. Tim's face was blank. He was here, but his mind and his heart were detached from the events at hand. This was a task that had to be carried out. There was no choice in the matter, like breaking the turkey's neck -- setting its head on the chopping block. It was necessary if a man wanted to feed his family, wanted them to survive. No one would give his people what they needed. They had to take it for themselves.

The little boy sat on the carpet in the emergency waiting room. He must have been five or six years old, tops. Tim watched him as he and his men passed by, their heavy boots thumping on the linoleum floor. The boy was playing with a metal fire truck, pushing it back and forth in place, making *"rumming!"* sounds to himself. The boy stopped short as he looked up, catching his breath. His awed expression, the sparkle of innocence in his eyes -- if Tim had any doubts about their mission, he would have felt them then. But he didn't. He couldn't. Besides, no one was going to get hurt, no one in this wing of the hospital, anyway. That wasn't part of the plan.

Tim caught Myer glancing at him from the corner of his eye. He clenched his teeth and walked faster. They were almost to the entrance of the Health Sciences Building.

***

"Sir, you have been receiving and spending very large checks from my organization for the last several years, and now, I would like to know where that money has been going!" Jeff spat out.

"If you'll listen to me, I can explain how your funding has been put to excellent use," Raj said, his heavy accent unfurling the words down the length of his tongue.

Nina stepped forward. "We've seen your usual progress *reports*. We're just interested in seeing some actual *progress-*"

"Well it doesn't work that way!" Raj interjected.

"Yes, it does," Nina shot back. "We're not the NIH. We can pull the plug if you don't cooperate."

They were standing at the entrance to Raj's lab. The one in the basement. Jeff looked around him. It was almost exactly like he had pictured it. Science-fiction-white hallways, brushed metal doorways and trim, double doors at the entrances to adjoining wings.

They entered the Department of Immunology's conference room at 12 o'clock sharp, and they were down in the labs ten minutes later. Jeff knew he had met this Gupta fellow before, but he remembered the guy's handshake immediately. Gupta's hands were dry and chapped. Scientist or not, this was never a good sign. Jeff took it as a warning that the guy's life was not in balance. Dry, irritated skin meant a lack of personal awareness, which meant a numbing to one's own comfort and position in the world, which revealed detachment from the physical, the immediate, which meant trouble. Detached people missed the simple things, the obvious facts. They were also much more likely to compromise their values, or rationalize actions that lead to tragedies. Some might have found Jeff's thinking a tad melodramatic, but that was okay, he could afford to be that way, and in his experience, melodramatic or not, he was usually right.

Raj had given them the tour, but he'd shown them nothing. He wouldn't take them into the back rooms. Jeff could see through the windows into the front of the labs, where workers in white coats bustled back and forth. In Raj's lab they'd been shown only a row of monkeys, each hooked up to a series of monitoring devices. None of the animals looked sick. They sat in their cages, IVs and catheters dropping from their bodies, clear plastic tubes fed through the metal bars of the cages. There appeared to be no research going on.

Nina was rattling off their demands.

"We're going to need a detailed report on your findings, the status of the project, and an explanation of where all of this is going before we'll release the next round of funding." She paused. "And we're going to need some video documentation and live demonstrations."

"These are highly unusual demands for a research grant," Raj sputtered.

"Like I said, we're not the government. This is private money we've been giving you, and in return, you need to give us a little information back. We need to know we're funding the right individuals and that we can trust the work you're doing."

Raj stared back at her, momentarily caught off guard.

"*Trust* the work that I'm doing?"

Jeff nodded.

"For all we know, you could be building a weapon down

here instead of a cure."

Raj paused for a moment.

"Are you cutting my funding?"

"Let's just say we're putting things on hold," David cut in.

"For how long?"

"That will be discussed," Nina said.

"Mr. Pepper," Raj stammered. "I am doing important research. Everything I've done has been relevant to the intent of your grant."

"I'm glad to hear that," Jeff responded.

"What do I have to do to make your happy?" Raj muttered.

There was a moment of silence, then Nina cleared her throat.

"Why don't we go upstairs and talk that over."

***

Morgan was breathing heavily now. She pressed her mouth against the side of his neck, biting into the skin as she tried to muffle her moans. He moved beneath her as she straddled him in the chair. They were both getting close. He tried to slow down, not wanting to finish before her. It didn't look like that was gonna be a problem.

She was moving faster now, shifting her feet to lift herself up and down. Nick held his hands on her hips, guiding her body over him, back and forth. They looked each other in the eyes as Morgan's lips curled into a sort of grimace -- a look of startled surprise, then a flash of concern as her teeth bit down on her lower lip -- then her mouth pulled up in a wicked smile.

"I'm coming."

"Oh, yeah?" Nick gasped back.

"Yeah."

Then she was leaning into his chest, digging her nails into his shirt as her movements slowed, and her body ground against him in spasmic, quivering bursts. She was kissing his neck and growing still when the fire alarms started going off. The sirens weren't nearby. It sounded like they were at the far end of the hospital. They were never for real anyways, the latest in a series of drills and false alarms. Half the time none of the faculty even left the building. What was the rush?

Besides, now it was his turn.

Morgan wrapped her arms around Nick's shoulders as he held her tightly and tilted her back and onto the floor. Morgan wrapped her legs around his back and pulled Nick deeper.

"Ohh, baby," she moaned softly in his ear.

Neither one of them heard the alarms after that.

***

Tim's right hand man, "Simon," walked out of a maintenance stairwell in the hospital's front courtyard and glanced around the corner. Dozens of people were rushing out of the buildings. He pulled out a two-way radio and marched around the corner. Like the rest of his men, all of whom were now flooding the building, Simon was dressed in full Seattle firefighter equipment.

The Surgery Pavilion was located in the hospital's east wing. That's where the alarms were going off. Simon didn't know the standard operating procedure if alarms should go off during surgery. Either way, it had to fray a doctor's nerves. Glad I'm not having bypass surgery, he thought to himself as he approached the front counter. Volunteers were wheeling patients out of the cancer clinic. The wheelchairs were mostly occupied by children, many of whom looked excited to see firefighters entering the building. Others looked too sick from treatment to even lift their heads. Simon brushed past one boy, probably in his early teens, whose hairless head and skin looked sore and red from chemotherapy. The boy sat slumped in a chair as a large middle-aged woman in medical scrubs wheeled him towards the exit. The woman looked up at Simon.

"Man, you guys are fast! The alarms *just* went off!"

Simon said nothing, just marched past her towards the western side of the facility.

The boy gripped the handles of his wheelchair and slowly tilted his head up to look at Simon's face.

***

Renoir hoisted a stack of paperwork and tapped it on the side of his desk. The first task of the day was taming the chaos of his work area. He was stepping down as chair of the department later that year, and the amount of work required for that transition alone was staggering. He had never been one for systems. His office was the picture of chaos. Piles and piles, and *piles* of paper lined every flat surface. The room was freezing cold. Stacks of paperwork blocked sunlight that might otherwise shoot its way through the windows, and papers covered every inch of ventilation. One day soon he'd get all of this cleared up.

In the meantime, his lucky cardigan sweater made up for any temperature problems.

At the moment, he was devising a scheme that involved arranging the paperwork in order of importance. In his mind, everything on legal-sized paper was unimportant. If it was of any value, it would be printed and bound in hardcover books. The discard piles were at the far end of his desk. They were getting taller by the minute.

He leaned back and let out a long sigh.

"Shit," he muttered.

That's when the alarms went off in the distance. Then, to Renoir's surprise, as he turned towards the entrance of his office, a man dressed all in black stepped into the doorway, raised a gun in his hand, and pulled the trigger.

MORGAN

Eventually, as the alarms continued blasting, they decided it was time to get out and look around.

They'd just done it again. The latest in their ongoing series of sexual exploits in the workplace. God it felt good. They couldn't help themselves. They didn't even try. It had been almost a year since they'd first gotten together. Yeah, she knew he was married, but the way she saw it, she and Nick were *together.* His "wife" hadn't called him in months. When they first met and started flirting with the possibilities of a relationship, he had tried calling Kendra constantly, but with only limited success. She was fucking someone else, Morgan was sure of it. Why else would a woman leave her husband on one side of the country, then resist his every effort to maintain the relationship? Morgan couldn't understand this, but then again, she couldn't understand many of her close female friends either. She had her personal aspirations. She didn't just leap into things with one guy, and then the next, but if she felt the pull between herself and a man, she felt *the pull,* an undeniable, unavoidable need to be with that person, intimately, almost violently. She'd felt that with Nick the first time she met him.

She'd come back to school early the previous fall (technically still summer) to set up a new apartment with a half-dozen girls she'd met through classes and her sorority. By mid-August they'd done the late summer rounds of Seattle. She'd gone to the parties, hung out with her girlfriends, messed around with the Greek guys she knew on campus. But there had been nothing serious. Nothing until the day she walked down to the Health Sciences Building on south campus, had an interview with one or two of the faculty for a student assistant position, then walked out into the hall, and in her nervous post-interview haze, had glided over to Nick's cubicle and seen him for the first time. He was certainly nothing special. His hair was short and sort of mussed, like he'd combed it fresh out of the shower, then forgotten to brush it again after pulling on his t-shirt. He was short, just an inch of two higher than her 5'6" build. He had the look of a once scrawny college runner, one who was having trouble adjusting to civilian life and was starting to get the tiniest signs of a bulge from too much sitting, and too much beer to ease the desk-job woes. She thought that was cute. But if one thing got Morgan on the hook from that first moment, it was his eyes. He had great eyes, deep blue, with little trails of darkness sliding back into the pupils. One glance and she was lying on her back in the grass, watching a bottle rocket as it trailed up into space, shimmering and shaking, the dark cone now the center of this man's eyes. Below those eyes were the marks of disappointment, the slightest wrinkles of age, or fatigue, that rose and fell along with the laugh lines at the sides of his mouth.

She knew she could get him to smile. She had her charms, and she used them. A flutter butterflied in her ribcage as she stepped forward, brushed her long blond hair back over her shoulders, and smiled. Her skin tingled. Her breath came easily. She didn't remember what she talked about, but it had worked. By the end, she'd reached out, put her hand on his arm, and known that she had him. Now she just had to find a way to extricate him from his disinterested wife.

The sex might help.

That had started quicker than usual, and it had been better than ever. First at her apartment. Then they'd gone away for a long weekend, a record-breaking weekend. Then, when waiting to go back to her place in the evenings had become unbearable, they'd started fucking at work. That was some of the best sex they'd ever had.

Was it illicit? Of course. Dangerous? In a way. But she didn't want to think it through too much, she just wanted to do it. And do it they had. She couldn't begin to count the number of times it had happened, or the number of hideaways they'd discovered while slipping away. Suffice to say, in a teaching hospital like the University, it was easy to find places to go at it. She'd just lean into Nick's cube, give him a look that said everything, and he'd follow her out the back door. A short, anxious walk through the building, then the switch of a lock, some fumbling with their clothes, and she was on top of him.

They'd just done it again.

Morgan stood, pulled on her panties, and walked over to Nick. She leaned down and gave him a long, lingering kiss.

The fire alarms continued ringing in the distance.

"Maybe we ought to pay attention to that," Nick said.

"I thought it was just a drill. It's always a drill."

"Sometimes it's not. Drills never last this long."

"All right then, lets go," she whispered with a wicked smirk. "I got what I came for."

She kissed him again, her teeth pulling softly on his lower lip. He stood, one hand on her back, and opened the door to the hallway. The sirens were blaring, but the hall was remained dark and empty. They stepped out into the open, their shoes tapping softly on the carpet underfoot.

"Do you think Jeff Pepper's gotten here yet?"

"He's supposed to be," Nick replied.

"Think he'll like Raj?" Morgan moaned.

"I sure as hell hope not."

Morgan reached down and took Nick's hand. His fingers wrapped around hers, giving them a squeeze. He shot her a look out of the corner of his eye. He loved her, she knew it. She wanted to take him away with her, or just back to her apartment - make a pot of coffee, curl up on the couch, and watch a movie. That would be nice. Quiet and intimate. He wasn't happy at work. She wasn't happy without him around. Unfortunately he had to work, and there was no point in her skipping out if he had to stay in this hellhole. So they walked on, and as they walked, a chill crept up Morgan's spine. She could see it in her mind, like the cartoon ice in a Bug's Bunny short, creeping and crackling down a thermometer as the mercury shot down, then exploded through the bottom. She could practically feel the ice crackling up each bony link in her back.

The sirens were ringing at the end of the hallway, in the hospital side of the building. She could hear someone speaking over the P.A. system, directing people out of the building. Yet on this side of the facility, in the research sciences wing, everything was silent.

"The alarms aren't ringing in this building."

"That happens sometimes," Nick responded.

"Do you have a funny feeling?"

"How do you mean?"

"Just, like, something isn't right."

"No."

They turned and walked into a stairwell. Nick pushed the door open with a *clang* that echoed through the concrete corridor. Again, all they heard as they walked down the stairs was the sound of their own footsteps.

"Guess we ought to split up again. Go in one at a time," Nick said flatly.

Morgan didn't respond.

They stopped at the bottom of the stairs outside the doors to the Immunology wing. Morgan stepped forward, wrapping her arms around his back. He looked down into her eyes.

"I love you," Morgan said slowly.

He hesitated. "You too."

They'd never said it before. Maybe it scared them, but it felt right. Then a slow kiss. Cool lips. Morgan took a step back.

"I'm gonna use the bathroom down the hall."

"I'll see you back there."

Before she knew it, he'd walked around the corner and out of sight. She took a deep breath, then walked through the doors and around the corner to the right, heading in the opposite direction. Her hands ran down the front of her shirt and around her waist, feeling to see if anything was askew. She knew more than a few people were onto their shenanigans, but modesty required that she at least attempt to keep up appearances. God, she was acting reckless. They both were.

Morgan knew from the *many* times they'd done this before that there was a little-used women's restroom just through the fire doors at the end of the hall. It felt odd walking into a building where the alarms were going off. In the distance, a voice was still directing people out of the building. Morgan walked to the heavy metal doors. For some reason they were still held open. Normally, even during a drill, the metal latches would have released to let the doors swing closed. These were still fixed open. It seemed odd. She hesitated as a strobe light flashed in her eyes from the ceiling overhead, then she stepped over the threshold, walked ten steps down the hall, and ducked into the women's restroom.

She closed the door behind her, locked it, and went into the stall. Something was gnawing at the back of her mind. She was never one of those alarmist girls, but she was starting to feel an unfamiliar panic.

She stood, flushed the toilet, and went out to the sink to wash her hands. Then, as she stood at the basin, looking into the mirror as she rinsed her hands under the cold water, she heard it.

Boom!

She jumped.

BOOM!

BAM. BAM.

It took her a moment to identify the sounds. The first image was of a wrecking ball bouncing off the side of the building. Her second thought was of the doors swinging shut in the corridor.

Maybe this *was* a fire!

She shut off the water and stepped out into the corridor.

The doors were indeed closed.

She ran over to them, and that's when it all changed.

She tried to force the double doors open. They moved a fraction of an inch, then stopped dead. She pushed harder. Nothing. She peeked down through the narrow pane of glass. A metal bar had been slipped through the door handles on the opposite side. A heavy bolt cut through the bar at a ninety-degree angle, holding it in place. A movement caught her eyes. Morgan peered down the hall through the window, where she saw two men in firefighters' uniforms carrying guns. Big ones. They were off to the side, half a hall length down, walking away from her. The men turned in her direction as she leaned her weight into the door. One raised his weapon, but the other put a hand on the his elbow, motioning for him to wait, nodding towards the locked doors. It made no difference. By the time they fired, Morgan would be gone. She pushed herself away from the door, turning in a half-circle, her shoes slipping under her as they fought for traction. Then she was off, running through the hospital, alarms blasting in her ears, the image of those men and the gun muzzles flashing in her mind. She thought of Nick, somewhere on the other side of those doors, and she ran faster.

***

Fire trucks were swarming the building now. Sam Ballard's eyes scanned the street as he expertly maneuvered his Blazer around the cars in front of him. The lights on the roof of his vehicle spun off around him, red and blue, then bounced back at him from the windshields of the surrounding cars. He cut the wheel from left to right sharply. Sirens blared from every direction, coming at him from side streets, from up ahead, and racing up from behind. Traffic was getting wild. Drivers didn't seem to know which way to turn next.

He'd been the fire chief for the University and the surrounding neighborhoods for the last ten years. About once a week, every week, every year for as long as he'd had the position, some sort of alarm had gone off at the college. They were mostly false alarms. Kids would pull them to watch the strobe lights going off like a Christmas tree from outside the building. New researchers would leave some damn thing roasting over a Bunsen burner 'til the sprinklers went off or the smell cleared the place out. Sure, there were one or two actual fires that broke out each year, but though he always told people to treat every alarm like an honest-to-God emergency, he admitted that more often than not, he and his men showed up in their gear, inspected the buildings, then reset the systems and filed a report for a false alarm.

Today felt different somehow. This didn't feel like another false alarm.

He swerved the wheel to the left and gunned the engine. Depending on which buildings were in question, they had set locations from which to direct emergency operations. This alarm was coming from the main facility, the heart of the hospital, from which a series of wings flailed outward. Sam would get to park in his favorite spot. The hospital had a valet service for hospital visitors coming to see patients. The entrance was a little half loop that branched off from the road in front of the building. A lot of people used the service when they came to take their loved ones home, too. There were numerous handicap-access ramps cut into the pavement. Sam turned into the loop. People were streaming out of the building; some looked confused, others scared. They were all on their cell phones. Sam aimed for a handicap ramp and stomped on the gas. His tires caught the edges slightly, but the Blazer forced its way up and over. He slammed on the brakes, his vehicle swerving slightly as his tires squealed to a stop on the sidewalk. There were probably some cool skid marks on the ground behind him, but unfortunately, there was no time to look. He hopped out of the cab and headed toward a police officer who had also parked on the sidewalk. The guy was in his mid-fifties, same salt and pepper hair as Sam, minus the walrus moustache. Mark Price, chief of police. Mark was talking into his radio as Sam approached. Just as Price looked up to say something to him, a massive explosion rang out behind them.

B-OO-M!

It felt about a block away. The ground rumbled beneath their feet. Sam looked over his shoulder at the huge construction crane hanging over the far wing of the building. A fireball roared up into the air, engulfing the crane's metal arm.

Mark's gaze followed the spires of flame that twirled up into the air. He raised his radio again, clicking the button and releasing a gasp of static.

"Guys, what the hell was that?"

***

Morgan was just rushing out the fire exits when she saw the accident. It was like something out of a movie. The crowd was pouring through the doors, then milling about in the building's courtyard. They were on the side facing the back driveway leading into the hospital, where the road looped down along Lake Union as it swept into the main parking garage. It was sunny. That was what caught her off guard. Amidst the fear of the events going on inside, after seeing two men with guns securing the fire doors upstairs, while her heart pounded harder and harder in her chest, as she realized that this was serious, *deadly serious*, amidst all of this, the sun had broken through the clouds and was shining on the crowd of people outside. People who probably assumed that everything was normal. Just another drill. The sunlight made her look up and follow the beams of light shooting down at the cars on the highway. Then she heard a truck slam on its brakes and turned to follow the sound of squealing brakes as everything around her slowed down. Morgan and the crowd could only watch in dismay as a line of cars stopped along the main road was slowly and methodically twisted, crunched, and plowed out of the way by a big rig truck, one hauling what looked to be a petroleum tanker behind it. Petroleum, gas, whatever it was, it had the little signs on the sides, the bright orange triangles with the dancing flames. Morgan heard herself gasp. A woman behind her screamed. Then the crowd started running for cover.

The truck's brakes shrieked as its tires locked up and skidded across the pavement. The driver pulled the horn as the tanker careened back and forth behind the rig, smashing into cars and sending them shooting off to the sides. The sounds of smashing glass and screeching metal were deafening. Then the driver either jerked the wheel too far to the side or lost complete control, for the truck took a sharp turn to the left, jumped the barrier in the middle of the road, and cut across the path of oncoming traffic, where it clipped a hatchback, sending the vehicle spinning ahead like a top. The little car's tires blew out a moment before the rig caught up to it, sweeping the car against its grill and driving it forward as sparks shot from the tortured rims. The car skittered back and forth against the speed before breaking free and spinning out to safety. The truck hopped the curb and picked up speed. Morgan caught a glimpse of the driver as he opened the cab door, leapt to freedom, and tumbled in the dirt a split second before the tanker's back tires plowed over his legs. Above the chaos, Morgan could hear the man's scream as the bones in his legs exploded.

The truck continued on, picking up speed now, seemingly possessed by a phantom driver, its front wheels turning back and forth wildly as it drove over the uneven soil. The tanker followed behind, its hitch twisting and pulling with each impact. All at once, the crowd saw where the truck was going and a gasp rose up from the mass of people. Construction crews were hard at work on the new wing of the hospital. The iron and glass skeleton of the new building stood a block or so away. Men in hard hats stood atop the half-completed structure, watching the truck in horror as it ran out of ground. The cab turned in

75

on itself, the bumper and grill digging into the dirt, sending a geyser of sand and gravel roaring up into the air.

Construction workers were running for cover.

Then-

Impact.

The briefest pause, and…

F-OoOom!

The tanker hit the back of the truck, twisted to the side, and slammed into the base of the construction crane that towered over the site. The tanker's metal skin peeled away as its jelly-like contents blasted out, then ignited. The explosion blew out what windows had already been installed. Flames engulfed the base of the crane, shooting up into the sky as the paint blistered away from the metal base.

Workers fled the building, running for safety and heading for the elevators at the far end of the site. The crowd behind the hospital watched warily, unsure where to go or what might happen next. Their eyes moved from the flames at the base of the crane to the massive arm that hung a dozen or so stories above them. The sounds of protesting metal began to fill the air, drawing the crowds eyes back to the base, now engulfed in fire.

Everyone started running.

***

Renoir didn't feel the bullet. It must have gone in and out in one clean motion, clipping him in the knee and causing one hell of a flesh wound. Hell, who was he kidding, it must have torn into something pretty vital, 'cause his leg was killing him. The bleeding was profuse. It didn't help that his assailant had forced him to walk on the injured leg and lead him to Raj's lab downstairs.

Raj, of course that fucker was the cause of this. Michel often joked that Gupta would be the death of him. Looks like he'd been morbidly correct. Now here he was, stumbling through his own department, leaning against the wall, the water cooler, anything along the way that could support his weight, as this man with an assault weapon followed behind him, shouting orders to a dozen similarly armed men in fire fighters uniforms. The men ran past the two of them and headed down a side hallway, where they split off, guns held at the ready.

"If this is a bank heist, you have your buildings mixed up." Renoir mumbled.

"Just get me to the labs sir!" Tim shouted.

"I'm doing my best. I could move a bit faster if you'd chosen a different persuasion method."

The man opened his mouth to speak, but stopped short at the sound of twisting metal. The noise rumbled through the building.

Tim ran to the windows as Renoir staggered behind. A wall of thick black smoke filled the air beyond the glass. It was the kind of smoke Renoir had seen in news footage during the first Gulf War, when fleeing troops had set fire to their own oil wells. It had been all the flames could do to keep up with the geysers of thick, choking oil as it spewed up from the ground and ignited. This was some sort of oil and gas fire. Flames roared up through the smoke. Renoir held his hand above his brow, trying to block the sunlight from his eyes as he looked down at the area below. He could see a fire truck to the north, circling around the main road in front of the hospital, coming down the back driveway that led to the main parking garage. A crowd to the south, in the courtyard behind the hospital, was starting to move down to the lake behind the building. Most of them were running. Some looked up in the air, an expression of terror passing over their faces, like the shadow of a cloud racing over the earth.

What were they looking at?

Renoir looked up, as did his attacker, this man Tim.

"Oh shit," Renoir said, at the same time his attacker sucked in a quick gasp of air.

The new wing of the hospital had been dwarfed by a construction crane for the last ten months. A *massive* construction crane. As he drove into the garage each morning, under the shadows of overhead beams being hoisted above, and as he left at night, again under the shadow of the hulking, silent beast, he'd often wondered what would happen if that piece of machinery should come down. Looked like he was gonna find out.

His captor watched the far end of the crane's arm, then his eyes shot down to the base, where a wall of flames danced around in a fiery ring. Flames crawled up the metal latticework, where strips of metal were curling and pulling away like footage from a time-lapse camera. The cries of tearing metal screeched through the windows.

That crane was definitely going to come down.

Renoir watched Tim's eyes as they moved from the base of the crane, back to the top, then swept downward. He, like Renoir, was calculating the arc its massive arm would follow should its base give way. They both came to the same conclusion.

"Is there a problem?" Renoir asked through tightened lips.

Tim turned to him, his eyes set, angry.

" You're parked in the garage, aren't you?" Renoir almost laughed.

Tim's hands tensed around the weapon in his hands.

The sounds of screaming metal rang out again as the two men turned back to the window, just as the crane gave way. It always surprised Renoir how much life could be like the movies. Big movies. This crane, this crane was *big*. And now here it was, collapsing under its own weight. The noise was cacophonous, a series of shrieks and moans that was only growing in intensity. Renoir's eyes pulled back in awe as the massive structure corkscrewed ever so slightly in place, then slowly began its fall sideways, towards the lake, towards the building's entrance and the main roadway. The people below ran for cover, while those on the north side watched helplessly as the crane pulled loose from its molten base and tore downward, through the air, through the surface of the roadway, and into the earth below, where it must have hit a series of gas and sewer lines, which themselves went up in flames, the explosions ripping up through the road every 30 yards, manhole covers and sections of roadway peeling off like blistered asphalt skin.

As quickly as it began, it was over.

The roadway was now completely obscured. What wasn't blocked in by the metal grillwork of the destroyed crane had been torn apart by the ensuing utility explosion. There was virtual silence, save for the sounds of dozens of car alarms going off inside the main garage. At his age, Renoir had seen a lot, but even this took the breath from him. He looked at his captor.

Renoir felt a tickle in his stomach.

Now they were *both* trapped.

Tim stared at the ground below, then clenched his jaw, turned to Renoir and motioned towards the door.

"Keep moving."

***

Jeff was trying to figure these guys out. They didn't look the way he might have pictured such men, but in his mind, they were undoubtedly terrorists. Was that a prejudice? Could you be prejudiced against terrorists? More often than not, wouldn't that make you prejudiced towards prejudiced people? The point was, he couldn't guess at the cause these men were fighting for, at least not based solely on their appearances. Maybe they were just after money. After all, except for the uniforms, which many of them had already removed, these guys looked like they could have been American businessmen. That's probably how the fuckers had gotten as far as they had.

He'd been watching them closely since the moment they'd taken control of the room, and he prided himself on the fact that their intrusion hadn't taken him by surprise, not in the least. The explosions outside raised eyebrows and Raj had sent one of his lab workers out to investigate, but the young man didn't come back alone. He'd returned moments later, shoved into the lab ahead of two men with guns. The momentum caused the young researcher to lose his footing and tumble to the floor in the middle of the lab. Jeff and David immediately stepped forward to help him to his feet, as roughly 10 other men, the ones in the uniforms, followed close behind. The last to enter the room was pushing an older gentleman ahead of him. Jeff heard Raj mutter "Michel" under his breath as the older man staggered inside. So that was Michel Renoir, the chair of the department. Jeff had read many of the man's papers over the years. They'd never met, but in all his publications, and in all Jeff had heard of his career, the overwhelming impression he'd gotten was of professionalism and character. Now here he was - Renoir - hobbling into the room, his pant leg stained with blood, a stain that was spreading rapidly.

Later, through whispered conversations in the corner, the group learned that a crane had come down - fallen across the road to the hospital's parking garage. That was the sound they'd heard. The *real* fire department was busy outside, trying to get control of the fire that had weakened the crane's base.

Tim and Simon were standing off to the side now, discussing something in muffled, staccato bursts. They weren't speaking any language Jeff could understand. He glanced at David and Nina, arching his eyebrows to ask, "Are you catching this?"

David shook his head.

Nina was straining to hear.

Jeff kept watching the men in the corner; then he studied the armed men around them. He was used to entering boardrooms and immediately sizing up the crowd, determining who was in charge, who wanted to be, and who would do anything for leadership. Because of Jeff's position, most people demurred to him automatically, which he found amusing, as his only qualification for such preordained hierarchy was his money. He'd been incredibly rich for the better part of his life, but it was only in the last decade that his business acumen and agility had caught up with the level of control his bank statements allowed him to flex in each of his financial associations. His assistants would scoff at what he truly felt had improved his powers of deduction, but he didn't care. That was the reason he had David and Nina on his staff. They employed the Harvard/Wharton business school principles on behalf of the Foundation, while Jeff got to play the part of the impulsive billionaire, who acted on whims, and ran his business dealings according to the principles of his sensei, Mr. Morita. He tried to imagine how sensei would size up the situation now. Jeff's eyes scanned the faces of the men around the room. The taller guy, with dark hair and the Jack Armstrong, all-American Boy look, that was clearly the leader. Tim was the name Jeff heard exchanged in the short mumblings among the group. What brief snippets of conversation Jeff picked up revealed a slight foreign accent, one he was still struggling to place.

The other man was Simon. He was blond, and about a foot shorter than his counterpart, but he looked as though he had more muscle to back up his actions. He seemed to be losing his cool a bit now. He was worried, while Tim seemed unflappable. Jeff studied Simon's eyes closely. The eyes were always the giveaway. Jeff knew where Simon's weakness lay and he knew how he could use it later. He tucked the knowledge away and moved on.

The rest of the room was another puzzle. Researchers, about a dozen of them, stood around the edges of the lab. None of them looked worried; they just looked irritated that their work had been interrupted. Their eyes gave up nothing.

The same was true of Renoir, who was leaning in the corner, holding one hand on his bleeding leg. Beads of sweat had sprung to the man's brow, but his expression showed no strain. His mouth was a relaxed, thin line. His eyes were clear. This was a man Jeff felt he could respect.

He looked at his associates. Nina and David. Jeff had once heard the three of them referred to as "The Brain" of the Foundation. He supposed his cohorts were considered the left and right lobes, while he was, what? The primitive brain? The id-controlling idea portion of the operation? That was fine by him. That was probably fine by everyone else as well, just so long as he kept signing the checks.

The description was dead on, however. Nina and David were the left and right regions of the organization's central core. Just watching them now, Jeff could tell what each was thinking. Nina stood in her business suit, hair just so, clothes just so, legs *just so…* Never mind. He wouldn't go there, not again. Maybe some day. She looked great, and the way her dark brown eyes were taking everything in, planning, strategizing, and extrapolating, well, it was quite appealing.

David seemed itchy to move. Jeff could see his fingers twitching and flexing behind his lightly clenched fists. The grip was loose, there was no white on the knuckles, but David was clearly ready for action. Jeff knew nothing stupid would take place, but it gave him comfort to see that one of them was thinking of revenge, especially when so many in the room seemed completely and hopelessly resigned to their fates.

Which brought him to Raj. Jeff had never liked the sound of the man. His personality had come through, even in his most technical project proposals, like the guy dotted every "I" and crossed every "T," but he never found any heart or passion to put into the words on the page, and so, they simply read like cold, calculating requests for more money. Raj's impersonal handshake was icing on a tasteless cake.

Now he was just standing there, head cocked forward like a mindless coat hook. His face looked peeved, like someone had just stuck a chilled olive down the back of his shorts. The cold-fish handshake was the clincher, though. That was the deciding factor. Once they got out of this, Jeff was cutting the funding. He knew it immediately. The way the guy was standing, the angle of the melon on his pencil neck, the vacant irritation in his eyes, and the way one hand was clasping the wrist above the other, line a ten-year-old cowering in the corner during gym class, that was it.

Jeff knew that look. Raj was someone who only looked out for himself. He was the kind of guy who never helped his buddies out in grade school. They might get tagged in the middle of a dodge ball match, and Raj might somehow survive, but he'd make no effort to help his friends out. He could be the only survivor, and he'd just stand there, all but closing his eyes, wishing the game was over, or daydreaming about his chemistry set back home. Well, now Jeff owned the man's chemistry set, and he was ready to smash it, or barring that, take it and give it to the fat kid, Milton, the one who knew nothing, but would mix everything together and make it explode. Ah Milton, you old goof.

Jeff's mind was wandering.

He looked back to Nina and David, who turned to him in

unison, their eyes calm and engaged. They were working on a solution.

Jeff walked over to them and leaned in an ear. Tim and Simon glanced over their shoulders at the three of them, then turned away. It was like the negotiating parties at a corporate merger. This would be interesting.

Jeff looked at Renoir. This man could fill them in on their predicament. When they got a chance, Jeff was ready to pick his brain.

***

Sam's men were treating victims at the scene of the explosion and trying to find out whether an operator had been in the crane's control cab when it went down. That would be the next, potentially gruesome bit of work they'd need to get out of the way.

The fact that the building was still at such an early stage of construction and free of landscaping had prevented the fire from spreading further than the reaches of its own fuel, but the breadth of the blaze was still massive. To someone just approaching the scene, the flames raging up through the clouds of thick smoke might have looked like some sort of gas-line explosion. The closest image Sam could conjure up was the long-ago news footage of the raging oil wells as Saddam's soldiers had retreated and set fire to drilling locations in the first Gulf War.

Sam had moved his base of operations from the front of the hospital to the hill overlooking the construction site. They were still determining the situation inside the building, but now he needed to keep one eye on the the incident on the lower grounds as well.

He raised a walkie-talkie and barked into the handset, "Any word on the crane operator?"

The radio crackled and hissed, then a voice hollered through the din. "Nothing yet. Frasier and Parker are talking to the crew now."

"Ten four," Sam responded.

A noise rose up from the crowd behind Sam as the forward-most people parted ways for Mark Price, who stepped forward, a young girl beside him. It was Morgan. Sam nodded his head towards them.

"What is it?"

His friend looked grim.

"We may have a different situation on our hands here."

"What do you mean?" Sam asked.

"This young lady says she was in the building and saw two men with firearms sealing off doors between the wings."

Sam turned to Morgan. "Is that true?"

She nodded back. "They were in fire department uniforms."

Sam felt a shiver. "Anyone else see this?"

Mark nodded slightly, "A few folks have mentioned seeing men in fire gear inside the building *before* the alarms went off. Did you guys have any inspections going on today?"

Sam shook his head. "No. And there were no calls to the station before then."

Mark put his hand on Morgan's shoulder. "Which area of the building were you in?"

"The Health Sciences wing."

"No alarms were set off in that section," Sam said.

"So there are probably still a lot of people down there." Mark pressed the transmitter on his radio. "This is Price. Tully, take a few men and check the entrance to the Health Sciences lobby."

"On our way."

Morgan's eyes were wide now. "What's going on?"

"We'll see in a minute," Mark barked.

Sam took a deep breath, the air in his lungs catching for a moment, then wheezing out in a series of staggered gasps. He was feeling the pressure.

Mark stood, two fingers lightly pressed against his chin. His eyes darted from side to side, a nervous tick, then they locked in place, and he turned to Morgan.

"Do you know if there was anything unusual happening on campus today? Any speakers or events?"

"Yeah-" Morgan started, her eyes opening wide. "Jeff Pepper was visiting the Department of Immunology."

"Jeff Pepper-" Mark glanced at Sam. "Why was he coming?"

"He's been funding some big project one of the research professors has been working on."

"What time was he supposed to arrive?" Sam asked.

"Noon."

"The alarms went off at 12:15," Sam said flatly.

"Shit."

The radio on Sam's shoulder crackled to life, "Chief, we have a situation here."

"What is it?"

A pause, then the hollow voice shot through, "It looks like we have about two dozen people in a hostage situation. The doors to the lobby have been sealed, 'bout a half dozen armed guys are standing guard."

"Oh my God!" Morgan exclaimed. "My boyfriend is in there."

Sam glanced at Morgan, then at Mark. "We have a VIP in a hostage situation, and armed gunmen in a government-funded research building... We're gonna have to step things up a bit."

"What does that mean?" Mark asked.

"I'm calling Ransom at the FBI."

***

The chopper was circling in around the south end off the building, giving them a clear view of the fire down below. Whatever had set off the blaze was still churning out a thick cloud of black smoke. A construction crane was on its side, debris spread down the hill and across a roadway behind the hospital. Masses of people were spread out in the areas around the site.

Brick Ransom sat by the window, the muscles in his arms and legs growing tense with anticipation. He was suited up in what he called his SWAT equipment, but where the movies always had the letters spread out across the back and chest of the outfit, his gear was plain black. Brick was 45 years old, and as they said in the movies, he should have been "too old for this shit," but he loved it.

The pilot's voice came through Ransom's earphones, "I'll have to sweep around to the north and land on the highway. That smoke's too thick on this side."

Ransom nodded his head.

Twenty minutes ago he'd been at home in his kitchen, slicing onions for a tartlet he was making for dinner. Tonight was the night of the "big date" with the woman he'd been seeing. Victoria. It was seal-the-deal night, which called for his signature seal-the-deal onion tartlet. Why it worked, he didn't know, but something about that dish, the flaky crust, the smell, the flavor. The fact that Brick, a muscular man's man, could put together such an intricate dish, it just seemed to work. Onion tartlet was his aphrodisiac of choice, an awesome force of nature he only pulled out when he knew he was ready for the next step. No point bedding a woman he wasn't looking to get serious with. That got too messy, and onion tartlet was just too complicated, no matter how hot the target. Plus, for a man like himself, there was always the risk of injury. Not to his heart, but to his hands. He worked fast, cutting and slicing, mincing and filleting. His hands and his eyes worked in sharp harmony, but on occasion, just as in his work, he would hit a bump and have an accident. His fingers were speckled with a series of small scars from long-ago wounds, mementos of dinners and work assignments gone by.

'Course, knives weren't the only utensils known to cause him harm. He'd jammed his fingers in guns. Blasted his skin with handgun discharge. And he'd shot more than a few guys, all bad, and in each case, the slip of his finger on the trigger had seemed almost serendipitous, like he'd read the culprit's mind and known the exact instant when he planned to turn the gun on the hostage, or open fire on the crowd below, and somehow he, Ransom, had popped off a round, hitting the bad guy, missing the good guys, and saving the day. No one ever suspected that he suffered from a sweaty trigger finger, but that was the case. He was working on that, but it always made him nervous. His greatest fear was being nicknamed Agent Butterfingers.

Victoria. He licked his lips, half for the woman, and half for the onion tartlet. God those things were good. One way or the other, he'd be home for dinner.

Back to the business at hand. The chopper was coming in for the approach. The pilot was scanning the area for power lines, carefully setting up the landing location.

"I'll have you on the ground in a minute."

Ransom glanced back at the other passengers onboard. There was Phelps, the top man at the Seattle FBI branch, perpetually dressed in a little plaid hat, with a John Waters moustache and Ed Harris features. Beside Phelps were Aftab and Murray, two guys similar to himself, dressed in the gear, ready to go into action. They were the action men, G-men with muscles and cool clothes. Then there was Brick Ransom himself, part action man, part negotiator, part improvisational decision maker. He liked to think of himself as MacGyver. He didn't tell people that. They'd laugh.

Then they were on the ground. A group of police officers headed up the lawn to greet them as the FBI contingent disembarked. The first officer stepped up, shouting over the spinning rotor blades.

"I'm Officer Gridley! Which one of you is in charge here?"

Phelps came forward. "Agent Phelps, Seattle FBI."

The officer looked at Phelps blankly.

"Which one of you is Brick Ransom?"

"I'm Agent Ransom."

"Follow me please, sir!"

Brick stared straight ahead, avoiding any sideways glances from Phelps, who was undoubtedly pissed off. The group headed down the sloping grass to the courtyard in front of the Research Sciences Building. Crowds of people, students and staff, stood in clusters everywhere.

Ransom knew there was a reason the police had asked for him and not Phelps. Actually, in this case there were several reasons. He was sort of the go-to guy for the Seattle Police Department. He was known to do good work with minimal hassle and maximum payoff. He was easy to deal with and made solid decisions. In this case there was another reason: He was good friends with Jeff Pepper. Jeff and the other fella, Mister Big Shot Computer Guy, they'd all gone to school together. Those two had been the computer guys, while Brick was the ladies man. At any rate, they were all kinda tight still. Brick had also helped each of them out in a number of delicate situations, the type that can only happen to two of the top-five richest men in the world. Kidnapping threats, ransom, extortion, all were scenarios both men had had to address at one stage or another over the last 10 years. They'd always come out on top.

When the police realized Jeff Pepper might in fact be in the middle of this particular crisis, they'd no doubt known there was only one man for the job: Agent Butterfingers.

***

The crane was blocking the exit. That's what Renoir was

91

telling them:

"The whole fucking thing came down."

Those were the words coming out of his mouth.

That was the situation.

These guys were trapped!

Jeff and the rest of the group stood huddled around Renoir, as the older man sat slumped in a chair in the corner, his hands clasped around his leg. Jeff squeezed his hand down on the old man's shoulder as David rolled up a blood-soaked pant leg to examine the wound. Renoir caught his breath between clenched teeth.

"Hold on," Jeff murmured to him.

Renoir turned away as David exposed the bullet wound. Blood was caking into a red and black plug, but a trickle of crimson swirled out and down the knee the moment the pant leg brushed against the wound. Nina caught her breath and pulled a scarf from around her neck. Jeff recognized it as the $600 Hermes he'd given her last Christmas.

"Here," Nina said. "Keep pressure on that."

"Thank you," Renoir responded, as he wrapped the cloth around his leg.

David rose from the floor, looking over at Tim and Simon, who were still conferring. It was a wonder the two hadn't stopped them as they huddled in the corner to talk. Tim had glanced over and nodded his head from his men to the group, and there had been some visible whitening of trigger fingers, but that was it. So far.

"Do you know why these guys are here?" David asked Renoir.

"Probably because of that asshole."

Renoir motioned to Raj, who stood off to the side, his right hand clasped around his left wrist, the two pulled against his crotch as if he had to pee.

"I suspect my *colleague* has created something that these men want."

"A vaccine?" Jeff asked.

Renoir scoffed, "Doubtful."

"I think what they want or don't want is beside the point," Nina interjected. "I'm more interested in what happens to us now."

The group fell silent.

"Well, it looks like for the moment, all of us, these guys included, are trapped in the building," Jeff said. "What would you do if you were in their shoes?"

"Well," Nina began. "Half the Seattle Police Department must be out there by now."

"We don't know that."

"Jeff, you might not think so, but to a lot of people, you're a pretty big deal. The police will be here, probably with half the FBI."

"Including Ransom?" Jeff's eyes brightened.

"Of course."

"Seriously though," Jeff started. "How would they know I'm here? How do we know if there are *any* police here yet?"

"They're here," Renoir said. "They responded to the fire alarms."

"The police did?" David asked.

"Police and fire. I could see them from the upstairs window.

They have the building surrounded."

Raj looked over, lifted his head curiously, and shifted his feet in place. Then a tumbler seemed to slide into place in his head and he wandered towards them.

"What the fuck have you been up to, Gupta?!" Renoir shouted.

***

Nick's footsteps echoed off the linoleum in the empty hallways. He'd been late before, and he'd certainly gone AWOL on more than one occasion, but this little rendezvous had run longer than usual. Not that that was a bad thing. Nick ran down the last corridor, rounded the corner, and slowed his pace to a medium clip as he walked through the doors into the office's back hallway.

It was quiet.

The place seemed abandoned.

He walked down the hall, looking into several of the faculty members' open doorways. The desks all sat empty. This was atypical.

He glanced over his shoulder at the door to the Chair's office. Renoir was no doubt coming in to greet Jeff Pepper upon his arrival. Maybe the entire department had left for a tour of Gupta's labs. A tour, coupled with a bit of ass kissing for additional grant money from Pepper's foundation. That was probably exactly what was going on. Still, maybe there was a delay. Maybe the faculty was just late, or Pepper was late, and Dr. Renoir was just sitting at his desk, checking his email, or playing video poker until he got the call to head downstairs.

Maybe.

Nick walked down the hall, paused at the doorway, then tilted his head inside. The blood was the first thing he spotted. Renoir's chair - spattered in fresh crimson. Blood darkened the side of the desk, sprayed over the wood in a fine mist.

All sound in the room swept into his ears. He heard his own heart beating as step by step he approached the desk and looked down at the floor.

There was no body.

That was good.

What there was was a pool of deep, deep red. Someone had been injured. He could only assume it had been Renoir. His senses grew sharper, though the room remained pin-drop silent. Nick looked at the pool of congealing liquid, then he looked closer, and saw that there was actually a trail. A blood-drop, drip pattern, spatter-paint trail of scientist blood. Here there were several drops leading to the doorway. A few feet further were several more. The gatherings grew thicker in spots, places where the victim must have stopped to gain his strength as he made his way out of the room.

Nick followed the trail. His heart beat faster with each crimson pool, which seemed to be more frequent as the trail progressed. The victim had not sat long after his injury. The wound was obviously bleeding faster as he went along.

Nick stopped at the window, where another red stain glistened in the carpet. Only now something else seized his attention. Through the window he saw the collapsed crane, the fire, the smoke, the crowds, the ambulances and trucks.

Something more than a fire had started while he and Morgan had been hiding out upstairs.

Nick ran for the stairs, throwing the door open in the concrete stairwell, where it echoed with a metallic *clang* behind him. He ran down the steps, his feet barely touching the tops - in a flash he was out in the downstairs hallway - running - running - then it all came together as he ran out into the main rotunda and caught his first glimpse of the situation - a flash of masked men, and gun barrels, and people with their hands on their heads, crouching on their knees, leaning on tables. Now he knew what was happening, and he slid to a stop, turning in mid-arc to head back from where he'd come, his shoes slipping and sliding beneath him as he raced frantically in the other direction, suddenly remembering all too clearly the dreams of childhood, where a stranger comes to get you, and try as you might, your legs just won't seem to move. Only Nick's legs moved. Slowly but steadily his sneaker treads caught hold, and then he was rushing away, his arms pumping, a silent scream wheezing from his lips as he heard people behind him, running after in pursuit.

***

"These blueprints are for shit," Ransom said.

He'd spread them out on the hood of a nearby squad car, and for the last 10 minutes had been trying to get some idea of how the building was laid out. A police officer in his early twenties approached him,

"Well, it's confirmed. Jeff Pepper's chopper landed on the roof at a quarter to noon."

"Thanks, but I knew that already," Brick shot back impatiently. The kid gave him a curious look, so he continued. "My gut told me, son. My gut told me."

The young officer struggled to keep from rolling his eyes as he walked away.

Brick looked back at the blueprints.

"These plans are bogus. If the University actually built this place from these things, then, well, then nothing, cause I don't believe it."

He looked at the girl who had been hanging around. She was a hottie, hotter than Victoria even. Well, a different hot, but-

"Hey, whats yer name?" Ransom barked.

"Morgan."

"Morgan, I need your help with these things. What I'm looking at here-" he pointed at the paper- "Isn't matching with what I'm seeing here." He looked up at the building.

Morgan walked over with just the right bounce and sway. Brick caught a whiff of her perfume.

College girl.

God she was hot.

Focus, Ransom. Focus.

Morgan looked at the plans carefully.

"Is this the front entry?" She circled her finger around the lower portion of the plans.

"Supposedly."

"Well, then this is where the department offices are-"

Ransom arched an eyebrow. She was smart, too...

"-and this, this is where the labs should be," Morgan

continued, pointing to a little illustrated teddy bear icon.

Ransom leaned forward to bring the plans into focus. His eyes were shot, but he didn't want this girl to see him in his readers.

"The labs are here?" he asked. "Where the school told the city they were putting in a daycare facility?"

Morgan shrugged her shoulders and nodded.

"Hmmm, looks like we have a little zoning violation here."

Sam Ballard walked over. "Stay on task, Ransom."

"I'm just saying."

Brick shrugged, turned his attention to Mark Price and Phelps, who were standing off to one side, arms crossed, discussing the matter seriously. They saw him looking and came over.

"We need to make contact with the people inside, find out what they want and see how the hostages are doing." Phelps said.

"And how will we do that? We don't even know how many of them there are, or who they've got in there," Ransom responded.

"We've got to assume the worst."

Price looked at Morgan. "It seems safe to assume they've got Jeff Pepper, so where would he be inside this building?"

"I'd try the Department of Immunology," Morgan said. "Or Dr. Gupta's "*daycare*" facility."

***

Nick ran down the hall and took a sharp left turn into the

maintenance tunnel.

He'd been through there twice before. First when he'd started at the University and was exploring the building during his lunch breaks. The second time when he and Morgan were looking for a warmer hiding spot when the weather took a chilly turn back in February. The first time he'd gotten about as far as the entrance to the furnace room before turning around and heading back to the regular hallway. The time with Morgan they'd gotten a bit further, actually finding a little back office, with a nice thick patio chaise cushion nestled into a warmly lit cubby. They hadn't really looked around much or considered how the place had gotten there -- it just looked like it didn't get much use -- so they'd locked the door and gone to town.

That room was what Nick was looking for now. If he could just get there, get inside, lock the door, and hide, then maybe, just maybe he could wait this thing out – whatever it was.

Jesus he was out of shape.

His feet were struggling to keep up with his body.

Maybe he'd shaken the guys behind him, but he could still hear their footsteps. They were barking things back and forth to each other. He couldn't tell what language they were speaking. He didn't care. What the fuck was going on?

The lights whizzed over his head like a caravan of flying saucers. The air in the tunnels was thick and wet. He could feel it belching in and out of his lungs. He tasted rust in the back of his throat.

The voices behind him were growing distant.

He'd outrun them.

Hopefully.

Now to hide and wait. Hide and wait.

His arms started flopping at his sides.

Gotta keep going.

Gotta keep going.

Run.

Gotta stop.

The hallway.

The door.

He'd found it.

Slipping into the darkened side corridor, Nick felt his way through the shadows, found the doorknob, twisted and pushed, stepped into the empty room, closed the door, slid the latch into place, and unscrewed the bulb. He slumped against the door, slid to the ground, and listened to his gasping breaths. Waiting for the sounds of footsteps.

Then sleep.

MAKING CONTACT

"What the fuck did you do, Gupta?" Renoir muttered as he shook his head.

Gupta looked at the floor and said nothing.

"These people are obviously here because of *your* research. Now tell us what it is you've been working on. It can't possibly be a vaccine for any disease. Terrorists don't come after folks to get vaccines."

Gupta looked up. "It might not be a vaccine, but it could be a cure."

"What the hell does that mean?" Jeff asked. "Do I even want to know what you've been spending my money on?"

"The Foundation's money," David interjected.

"It's my money, David."

"Sometimes, the only way to abolish something is... to destroy it," Gupta stammered. "Once a disease has been defeated, one of the most common questions is whether the samples should be destroyed too."

Pepper looked at him blanky. "Is this a joke? I didn't grant your lab this money to find a way to destroy this virus. The idea was to save people."

"And it might-"

Jeff stepped forward. "And what did you come up with?!"

Nina put her hand on Jeff's shoulder, pulling him back. "Jeff. Calm."

Jeff shrugged her hand away.

"Don't kid yourself, Raj." Renoir spat. "You don't think what you've done is right, do you? I can see it in the way you're acting. I hear it in your voice. You've stopped strutting around like a rooster, the way you usually act when you sense the Nobel is within reach." Renoir's face was growing red, even as his features fell in pain. He squeezed his hands around the bloody fabric on his leg. "Hell, you've been as secretive as a White House flunky."

"And about as competent," Jeff added.

Gupta was quiet.

"Listen, we've got to remember two things here. Three if you really want to get into it," David hissed. "First, these guys are here for a reason. They didn't come here to hole up in the building all day. They want to get in, get what they need, and get out. Second, the place is surrounded with police and fire, which means these guys have their backs to the wall. The longer they wait to make a run for it, the harder it's gonna be for them."

"And what's the third thing?" Jeff asked.

"The third thing is *you*."

"What about me?"

"You're the ultimate monkey wrench. Once they find out who you are, who knows what their plan will be?"

"That might not be such a good thing!" Jeff said sharply.

"He's right though," Nina interjected.

Jeff's mouth tightened. "Who gives a fuck who I am? We're all in this together. Sooner or later we've got to convince these guys to leave us here and hit the road."

"What do you think they're waiting for?" Nina asked. "What do they need before they can go?"

"What we *need?*" Tim's voice echoed behind them. "What we *need* is a demonstration."

The group looked at him. He and Simon had crossed half a room's length toward them.

"A demonstration of what?" Renoir asked.

"You know very well what. Dr. Gupta's little invention here. My new tool."

"Tool, or weapon?" Renoir replied, his eyes again locking on Raj.

"Whatever you prefer. Just so long as it works."

"It works." Gupta said.

"So I've been told, but I need to know for sure."

"Then use it on one of your buddies here," David said with a nod towards the gunmen by the door.

"Well now, that wouldn't make much sense," Tim said, tapping his fingers on the side of a workbench. "I was thinking of using it on the good doctor, but maybe I'll just test it on you."

David froze, and Jeff stood up. "For fuck's sake, stop talking and just get the hell out of here with the stuff, whatever the hell it is."

Tim looked at him coldly. "My, my. Calm yourself, sir. Maybe you'd like to be the guinea pig yourself?"

***

"So we know Pepper was meeting with Raj Gupta today-" Ransom was pacing back and forth in front of the building blueprints.

"And Gupta's offices are in the wing that's now locked down," Phelps continued. "Should we assume there's a connection?"

Ransom looked up. "You thinking a kidnapping, ransom situation?"

"It seems like a possibility."

"So, what do we do? Wait for them to contact us, or start calling every phone in the building?"

"Well, lets go about this logically. If he was meeting with Gupta, lets call the places Gupta would be." Phelps turned to Morgan. "Do you know any of Gupta's office and lab numbers?"

"That cheapskate?" Morgan snorted. "Are you kidding me?"

Phelps and Ransom waited for her to finish.

"I know them all," she went on. "He'd always have me call his relatives on the school number and patch him in so he didn't have to pay for long distance from home. When he's traveling he always calls the toll-free numbers and has us forward the calls to his labs so he doesn't have to use up any grant money."

"And what are the numbers?" Ransom asked, as he held up his cell phone.

"34545 and 31955," Morgan rattled off.

Ransom started typing them into his handset.

"Hold it Ransom," Phelps stepped in. "I'm still in charge here. I call."

***

Jeff stared the man in the eyes. "You wanna test it on me? Go ahead."

"Suit yourself," Tim responded.

Tim nodded towards Pepper, and two of the men by the door came over, putting their hands on Jeff's shoulders and pulling him towards the middle of the room.

"Dr. Gupta," Tim continued. "We'll need your help on this."

Gupta caught his breath, then rose unsteadily to his feet.

"Where have you been placing the test subjects?"

Gupta pointed to the far end of the room, where a glass panel looked in on a dimly lit white room with a single stool inside.

"Put him in there," Tim grumbled.

The two men followed Tim's orders. Jeff's body went rigid, but he didn't fight.

"You're making a mistake," Jeff said through gritted teeth. "You don't need to test anything. You just need to get the fuck out of here."

"Plenty of time for both," Tim replied.

"I don't think so."

"If the doctor's results work as well as we've heard, we'll have plenty of time to spare."

Tim walked over to a thick door at the end of the room, looked down at a panel of keys by the handle, then pushed a single green button. The door opened with a soft hiss of air, and the men started pushing Jeff inside.

"Might as well loosen your tie and get comfortable," Tim said as he walked away. "Dr. Gupta, close the door and get started."

Gupta moved slowly, gathering his wits about him. He approached the portal slowly, reaching up with his hand-

"Gupta! You're a fucking coward!" Renoir shouted at him.

"You're kissing your career goodbye," Nina added.

Gupta hesitated, then pressed his hand against the door and swung it closed. Jeff glowered at him through the thick glass.

Then, the phone started ringing...

***

Tim lifted the receiver from its cradle on the wall. He said nothing, simply held it to his ear. There was an ever-so-soft click on the end of the line, then a voice came on, a sort of older brother, commanding, yet jovial voice, one with an oh-so-subtle southern lilt at the end of each word.

"Hello," the voice said.

The tumblers in Tim's brain skittered softly as he looked around the room.

At the moment he had two businessmen, a woman, two professors, and three lab techs held captive. Three of his men: two gunmen and his second in command, Simon, were placed at the doors and pacing the room. Upstairs, from what Simon had just told him, there were a dozen more hostages, and almost as many of his own men holding them and guarding the main rotunda.

Their exit was now blocked. They needed to find another

way out.

Of course, there was also that wall of canisters on the far side of the room. Each was the size of a beer bottle, white, with a small blue rocker switch on the side. One click, a few electric pings, and everything would be different.

Those canisters were the wild card.

He contemplated them. Which would be the easiest to lift? Where would he hide it? Were they heavy? The variables made his heart stutter, but only once. His eyes darted to the side and he saw Professor Renoir looking right at him, his expression set, his mouth a thin line. Their eyes locked, then Renoir looked away.

"Is this the man in charge?" the voice on the phone continued.

"Yes it is," Tim answered softly.

"Can I get your name?" The voice questioned.

"You can call me Tim."

"Tim, this is agent Phelps, from the Washington State FBI."

"Yes?" Tim waited.

A moment of silence as Phelps undoubtedly consulted with his cohorts as to what he should say next.

"Do you have a moment to talk, Tim?"

"Only if you can help me."

"We're here to help. That's why I'm calling," Phelps said. "You've obviously got something underway here. I don't know what, so I need you to fill me in on some things."

Again, Tim sat silently.

"It might help us if you'd explain why you're doing this, what you're after."

"Just doing an errand, picking up a few things."

"Uh huh..."

He could hear Phelps' brain churning.

"Well Tim, it looks like while you were in the store, getting the milk or whatever it was you were after, something blew up in the store parking lot, if you know what I mean."

"Yes, I've been made aware of that," Tim said coolly.

"Does that affect your plans at all?"

"I'm working on that."

"That's what I was figuring," Phelps drawled back. "Thought we might be able to help you out with that."

"Look, agent-"

"Phelps."

"Look agent Phelps, I've got your number here. Perhaps I'll get back to you in a little bit-"

"Fine."

"-and you know where you can get ahold of me now."

"Yes I do," the voice said flatly. "One more thing."

Tim waited. He heard Phelps take in a shallow breath.

"Does this have something to do with Jeff Pepper? Is he all right?"

Tim's eyes settled on the man standing on the opposite side of the glass.

Son of a bitch.

He heard another breath on the end of the line, "- - -."

Then he hung up the phone.

***

"Well good job buddy," Ransom patted Phelps on the back. "You either saved my friend's life, or signed his death certificate with that last comment."

Phelps ignored him. He glanced at Murray, who stood over a field computer waiting for results. A green *"Fantasia"* voice line danced on the screen as Tim's muffled voice was replayed through the machine's tiny speakers.

"You get anything yet?" Phelps asked.

"We've got a couple possible matches. Narrowing it down as we speak."

Ransom was getting worked up. "What do we do now?"

"You know what we do now. You've been through one or two of these before." Phelps continued. "This is where we wait."

"Where we wait." Ransom flexed his hands. "Wait to find out if we're calling the bio cleanup crew, going in to do something ourselves, or standing out here with our respective thumbs up our asses? That kind of waiting?"

Phelps nodded, "We *do* work for the U.S. government, son."

Brick had no comeback.

They waited.

The fire department was slowly getting the fire at the construction site under control. Three hoses were spraying at the base of the flames as steam rolfed up into the air in thick, white plumes. An ambulance squawked its siren as it made its way from the accident site to the far end of the hospital.

"That's convenient," Phelps observed as the vehicle drove past.

"Okay," Murray said. "We've got a couple of possibilities, but one with a 90 percent match." He pointed at a couple of spikes in the line chart.

"And who is that?" Ransom asked.

Murray's fingers flew over the keyboard as he pulled up a series of windows. Then he tapped the keyboard once and a voice came through the speakers:

" I believe our negotiations are wrapping up now. Perhaps next time you'll try harder to make this work for both of us-"

The recording cut off abruptly.

"What happened there?" Phelps asked.

Murray made a mushroom cloud gesture with his hands, *"Boom."*

"When was that?"

"U.S. Embassy bombing in one of our pet countries. Three years ago. He and his crew took control of the building with 33 Americans inside. Made their demands, got half of them filled, then got restless. Wiped out half of his own guys in the process. He and the main group escaped through the parking garage, slipped into the crowd during the explosion."

"What kind of an explosion?" Phelps asked.

"A big one."

Ransom looked at his boss, his face a virtual question mark.

Phelps shrugged his shoulders and turned to Murray. "It's not a stupid question."

"Well, it wasn't a dirty bomb, but it was strong. Turned a five-story building to pancake mix in about 15 seconds."

"Who is he?" Ransom asked.

"Last name's Griffin. First name they don't know. Initials

on file are H. K."

"What group is he with?"

"Near as we can tell, he's a free agent. All his tags are for weapons connections. He seems to set the bad guys up with their nasty little toys, but he's got that mean streak. There are three big events in here, and all of them ended with him killing the hostages despite the result."

"So he's spiteful?" Phelps said. "Great."

"How sure are you on this match?" said Ransom.

"I'd love visual confirmation." Murray turned the computer to show a picture of an average looking guy with a close-cropped haircut on screen. "But even without it, I'm pretty sure this is him."

"So, we won't expect negotiations to play out in good faith."

"Don't let him think that, though!" Phelps grumbled. "Jesus."

"But this *is* who we believe we're dealing with?" Ransom asked.

Phelps nodded.

"Okay then." Brick turned to Murray. "Talk to your guys, get me everything you can find on this guy. I need to know what I'm dealing with."

"What we're dealing with, Ransom," Phelps muttered. "What we're dealing with is-"

His words were wasted. Ransom was already headed for the squad car, returning to the spread-out building plans.

***

Jeff was still standing in the middle of the glass-enclosed room.

He looked bored.

It was a façade.

His mind was racing. He looked at Tim, who had just hung up the phone. He couldn't hear a word that had been said. Nina and David's expressions showed mutual confusion.

Who had this guy been talking to?

More of his cohorts? The police?

What would happen now? Were they about to see Raj's project in action? On himself?? Jesus.

Tim's hand still rested on the phone receiver as it sat in its cradle on the wall. He brought two fingers to the bridge of his nose and squeezed the skin between his eyes, massaging it sharply. Then, just as casually, Tim approached the glass and pulled the door open.

"Mr. Pepper, please make yourself comfortable."

Then he turned and walked out of the room, leaving his men behind to stand watch.

The group sat, bewildered, as Jeff walked out of the chamber and back across the room. He shrugged his shoulders, not knowing what to do next.

Then he realized.

The guy knew who he was now.

That could only be a bad thing.

INSIDE STORY

The news vans were starting to arrive at the scene. Brick watched as they hopped the curb and pulled up alongside the police and fire department vehicles.

What made the media folks feel they were just as important as the people trying to handle every crisis?

The van for KOMO News was the first to open its doors, and a heavyset guy in a Hawaiian shirt emerged from within, carrying a camera in his left hand. He lurched his legs out, one then the next, and stumbled onto the sidewalk, where he sort of teetered backwards as he closed the doors behind him.

A blond-haired woman in her early thirties sat in the front seat, poking at her hair with a pick. Brick leaned forward, getting a better look to confirm his suspicions.

Yep.

Hot.

The guy in the shirt looked over at him.

"Hey man! What's happening?"

Brick shrugged his shoulders. "Beats me."

"Come on man, look at you. You're wearing the gear; you

know what's up."

Brick shook his head slightly, but smirked.

The fat guy put out his hand. "Dub Taylor, KOMO News."

"Brick Ransom, FBI."

"FBI huh?"

"I still can't tell you anything," Brick replied.

"Well, can you at least suggest a good spot to shoot from? I need to get this thing rolling so they can cut to us from the studio."

Brick studied the camera, then turned to the bay of windows along the second floor of the Health Sciences Building.

"Hey, what kind of range does that camera have?"

"Let me put it this way. With the zoom on this thing, I could make a fortune selling videos of the sorority girls here on campus, and I live way up on Queen Anne."

Brick nodded. "Follow me."

***

Nick's eyes popped open.

His chin shot up from his chest and the back of his head thumped against the door. He'd fallen asleep, just for a moment. A moment, or an hour, he couldn't tell. The room was pitch black. He blinked and looked around. A thin band of pale light glowed at the base of the door. The details of the room began moving forward through the darkness as his eyes adjusted. He wanted to turn on a light, but he didn't dare.

A hollow, metallic rumbling grumbled overhead. The ventilation ducts were shifting as the air came on. Maybe he could climb through those to safety.

Nah, that only worked in the movies.

In real life it would be like *The Breakfast Club* -- even if he *could* wedge himself in there, the whole damn thing would come tumbling down as soon as he crawled out over the hallway. What good would that do him? He'd get shot up like a fish in a barrel.

Nick lowered his head to the floor, listening for noises from down the corridor.

Silence.

What the hell had he gotten himself into here?

Yeah, he'd run away, but run away to a private prison cell in the basement of the building. There were no ways out of here. No windows. No escape hatches. Just an empty room, with a locked door, and an unscrewed light bulb. He stood up, feeling his way though the darkness, his hands skimming over the painted cinder-block walls. Maybe there was a fire axe or a broom or something.

Then he felt it. He almost knocked it off the wall as his hands swept up and down like a blind man's.

Screw the light bulb.

He had a telephone.

***

The phone rang again.

Phelps answered and walked to the side of the curb, covering one ear from the sounds of the people around him.

The scene was growing more carnival-like by the second.

115

The news vans from several TV station were set up now. Every 10 yards, a young, blond reporter was delivering a similar shpeel. Morgan watched from a distance as the woman from KOMO News rattled off her variation on the events of the afternoon.

"This is Rebecca Frasier, live at the scene of a bizarre police, fire, and state law enforcement operation at the University campus here in Seattle. No word yet on what exactly has taken place, but we'll be sure to keep you posted. In the meantime, check out this shot of a burning tanker truck and a construction site engulfed in flames."

The camera guy, Dub, quickly panned the camera over to the slowly dying fire at the base of the hill as Ms. Frasier lifted her hand to her ear, no doubt catching the entrancing insight of the anchors back at the station.

Rebecca nodded her head, "Yes, *fire*. Lots and *lots* of fire. Mmm-hmmm... mm-hmmmm, well, no word on the situation at the school itself, but yes, the FBI is here, and there are individuals in what appear to be SWAT uniforms arriving on the scene."

As if on cue, three black vans came roaring down the street. They came to a stop in front of the building, and three dozen men in dark assault gear came bursting out onto the sidewalk. Morgan watched, agog, as the men swarmed the scene, two of them rushing toward Phelps, who waved them away with his hand. Morgan stepped closer to see what the FBI lead was discussing. The other guy, Brick Ransom, (what a *hottie,* and what a name!), he too was watching Phelps closely as the man spoke into the handset.

"Are we sure this isn't some type of practical joke? The news guys are showing this place from every angle at the moment. This could be some asshole with too much time on his hands between *Jerry Springer* and his daily *Girls Gone Wild* video fix."

Phelps nodded his head.

"Okay then, patch him through."

Phelps looked at Ransom.

"What is it?" Ransom asked.

"911 just got a call from a man claiming to be inside the building."

Morgan's head shot up.

"They're patching the call through to me now," Phelps continued.

Ransom spun towards Aftab and Murray, snapping his fingers and motioning for them to record the call. Murray nodded and turned to his computer.

There was a pause as Phelps stood there with his mouth hanging open slightly, waiting to speak, "- - -."

The phone clicked audibly.

"Hello. This is Agent Phelps from the FBI. Who am I talking to?"

Morgan held her hands to her chest, afraid to breathe. Ransom glanced over, seeing the expectant expression on her face.

"Nick King?" Phelps asked.

Morgan let out a sigh of relief.

"That your boyfriend?" Ransom asked.

Morgan nodded.

Brick didn't know why, but he was sort of pissed off.

"Okay Nick, first of all, are you all right?" Phelps nodded

his head. "Good. Good. Then we're gonna need to get some information from you."

Morgan shivered as her arms and legs started trembling. She sat down on the curb and looked over at Ransom, who had turned and was now walking over to the KOMO cameraman. She looked up at Phelps, who was looking off into the distance as he spoke into the phone.

"First of all, lets start with where in the building you are right now."

***

"I'm in the utility tunnel on the first floor."

Without realizing it, Nick had pressed his back into the corner of the room, trying to squeeze himself into the tightest, most protected place he could find. He held the phone against his mouth, speaking into the mouthpiece with a hushed hiss.

"I don't know what's going on here, man, but there are gunmen in this building."

"We're aware of that, son." Phelps said.

"I was in another part of the building when the alarms went off. My girlfriend was with me. Her name is Morgan Phillips."

There was a pause.

"Morgan is here with us, Nick."

Nick's breath caught in his throat. "She is?" He exhaled in a series of stammering gasps. "Thank God."

Phelps continued, his southern drawl dripping through the handset. "Son, we're not sure what the hell is going on, but we're hoping you might be able to give us a little more information about what's happened in there."

"I'll try."

"We don't know who these people are, or what they want. We don't have a clue, so we don't know how to deal with them yet. If they'll negotiate. If they just want to get out. If they're there to take lives."

"There was blood," Nick said.

Phelps stopped short, "Blood-?"

"In the Immunology Department office."

"Did you see any victims?" Phelps asked. "Any bodies?"

"No."

"Have you seen anyone?"

"Yeah. I had to run from two men. They saw me as I was heading downstairs to get out of the building."

"So, you're near the front rotunda?"

"I was. I'm a little ways away from there now."

"Can you hear anything?"

"Not really."

Nick was trying to slow his breathing. He strained his ears, listening, trying to picture the corridor in his mind, mentally walking through the halls and out to the rotunda where he had seen the men with their guns, and the hostages.

"We know these people have hostages in that part of the building. Were you able to get a look at them? Could you see who they have with them?"

Images flickered through Nick's mind. Backpacks and laptops. An iPod smashed across the floor. He saw the lady from the lunch line slumped against a wall, her hands held to her face.

"There are mostly students, some of the people who work

downstairs."

"How many do you think they have?"

"Maybe a couple dozen."

"Did anyone seem hurt?"

"Look, I'm sorry, I really can't say."

There was a long pause. Nick could hear muffled voices conferring on the other end of the line, then Phelps' voice came back through.

"Nick, we may be asking you for a little help in a bit. Would you be able to do that for us?"

Nick felt sweat pop from his forehead. "I can try."

"Good. Good." Phelps paused a beat. "We've got someone here who'd like to talk to you now."

"Okay."

The sound paused again, then Morgan's voice came through. "Baby, is that you? Are you all right?"

Nick's heart started racing. "Yeah babe, I'm fine."

***

Phelps walked away as the girl began speaking breathlessly into the telephone. Ransom was patting the camera guy on the back and pointing to the bottom of the hill. *What in the hell was he up to?*

"Ransom!" Phelps shouted. "We've got someone in the building."

Ransom looked up and headed towards him. "Who?"

Phelps jerked his thumb back over his shoulder. "Girl's boyfriend. He got to a phone inside."

"What could he tell us?"

"Not much. I thought we might be able to use him though."

Ransom nodded his head, thinking.

"What's your friend doing?" Phelps motioned to Dub Taylor, who was staggering down the hillside with his camera in tow.

"I thought he might be able to get us some footage through the front of the building. Maybe get some shots to confirm who we're dealing with."

"You trying to get us brought up on charges of endangering civilians?"

"Relax," Ransom sighed. "He's a cameraman! This is what they do."

Phelps started to speak, then stopped short as he saw the heavy-set guy setting his camera up on a set of steps that sat at an angle across from the building. The guy was in horrible shape, his belly swelling up over the top of his belt, his leg's jiggly and soft, like packaged biscuit dough. Without his jeans, this guy had to look like the doughboy.

Wait, he wasn't actually setting up the camera's tripod, he was leaving it behind as he shouldered the camera and headed for the building.

"What is he doing?" Phelps hissed. He motioned at the guy and shouted, "Stay away from that building!"

Taylor either ignored him, or he was out of ear range. Nevertheless, he continued on, making his way down the length of the steps, then hanging close to the side of the building, where he shimmied down as best he could, his back pressed against the brick wall, and began filming. He played with the controls, trying to get the best angle and exposure. The sun was glinting off the glass face of the building. Through the entry way -- which was two automatic sliding doors, then a walking space, then two more doors -- he could almost, *almost* make out the silhouettes of people inside, but he couldn't see if they were captives or hostages. Dub shielded his eyes from the light and glanced back at the group of agents clustered at the top of the hill by the street. Phelps threw up his hands, sweeping them back and forth in front of his face as he mouthed the word "No!" Ransom on the other hand stood behind his superior, his arms crossed, expression blank, and nodded once. Dub stood up and shuffled along the wall, moving closer to the building.

Phelps spun his head around, glaring at Ransom. "What did you tell him to do?"

"I just thought it might be in our best interest to get some footage of these guys. See if we can get a view into the rotunda to see what we're dealing with."

"So you sent an overweight camera guy from the local news station?! Are you out of your mind?"

"He's got a better camera than us. Plus, he asked me if he could do it. He's looking to win some press awards."

Phelps shook his head. Un-believable.

Taylor was down to the corner of the building now, where the brick western wing butted up against the glass wall of the Health Sciences Building. Again, he looked up the hill, where the police, fire, and FBI stood in clusters, all watching him. Students and other civilians were spread out along the sidewalk by the street, hundreds of them. No one was talking or shouting, or spreading first-hand accounts of the events over their cell phones. Everyone was watching him.

Great.

What had he gotten himself into?

His palms were starting to sweat. Suddenly his grip on the camera and the controls seemed tenuous at best. He crouched to the ground and tried to catch his breath.

"Now or never Dubby Boy. Now or never."

Leaning back on his heels, he pushed the record button on the camera, manually turning the focus ring as he looked through the viewfinder. At first he saw nothing, only sun glare and blurs; then he leaned into the shadows of the building, zoomed in past the glass and the outside light, and jostled the controls.

Pop.

He had a clear shot inside. Could see all the way through to the far side of the building, where four guys were standing watch. In the center of the rotunda were about two dozen tables, at which students and research staff sat in clusters. Some of them were crying, hunched over the tables as their companions put their hands on their backs and leaned down to talk to them. A row of students sat on the floor, their legs pulled up to their chests, heads fallen back against the wall. For a second it looked to Taylor like this last bunch might be dead, gunned down all in a row. Then one of them moved, rubbed his face, and leaned over to talk to his neighbor. This caught the gunmens' attention. They looked back at the hostages, then over to three more men who stood along the front entrance.

Dub continued filming. He was a dozen or so yards from the northern entrance. The gunmen seemed more interested in watching the people in the rotunda than they were in seeing what was happening outside. Then, as Dub continued filming, the movements in the room changed suddenly. The gunman near his entrance stood at attention, as did the men at the other end of the building. The hostages looked around quickly, some huddled up against each other. Dub pulled the zoom back, sweeping the camera's angle around the interior of the building, trying to catch a glimpse of what was happening. He swept back and forth. Back and forth. Then he stopped. A group of three men came walking into the rotunda from a side corridor. From the way they moved, these were clearly the brains of the operation, the guys in charge of all this. One of the men, an average looking guy with dark hair and a thick, furrowed brow, was clearly the leader. He came in, looked around the room, then turned and started for the guards near Dub's end of the building. Holy shit! Dub rocked the zoom all the way forward as he turned the focus ring. Fuck. His knees were killing him. He tried to shift his weight. Ouch. Keep filming, Dub, keep filming! He got a couple more seconds of footage, then paused and moved forward a bit. No sooner did he shift his weight, than he knew it was a mistake. The lens crept out of the shadows, the ones that were helping him get the shot he wanted, and tilted out into the sunlight, sunlight that ever so briefly flashed off the glass and reflected into the building. Dub caught his balance as he looked through the lens again and into the room. The guy in charge was looking up now - *furious*. He was pointing towards the front of the room now. At the windows! At him!

Rattatatatatata!

Boom!Boom!Boom!Boom!Boom!Boom!Boom!Boom!

Dub grabbed his camera by the handle and took off running.

The glass around him exploded into a wall of twirling glass shards. He could see pieces of pavement and chunks of dirt rippling up off the ground as a barrage of bullets skittered back and forth. He fell backwards and heard the camera hit the ground with a hollow *chunking* noise.

Shit, that would cost him. But not as much as if one of those bullets hit him.

"Gah!"

He crawled behind a concrete planter that ran along the front of the adjoining building. He pulled his arms and legs behind the cover and looked down at his side. A plume of blood was seeping through his shirt.

Ransom looked down on the action, caught off guard by how quickly all hell had broken loose. He motioned to the SWAT team that had moved in on the front of the building the minute the gunfire rang out.

The men swarmed down the hill, moving in single file along the edge of the front lawn, then fanning out at the bottom, each officer falling to one knee behind the bike lockers and utility boxes in front of the building. They opened fire on the gunmen who were shooting out into the crowd. The hostages inside the building started screaming. The crowd outside the building echoed the shouts of terror as they scattered down the street, away from the chaos.

Ransom ran down the hillside, his feet nearly losing their footing as they tried to keep up with his body. He got to the bottom and dove for the ground, rolling over the concrete walkway and slamming into the side of the concrete planter, about fifteen feet from where Dub was lying. He looked up at the heavy-set man, whose mouth was starting to quiver as he threatened to go into shock.

"Hang in there, Dub!" Ransom shouted at him.

Dub looked back at him weakly.

Brick started crawling on his elbows and knees, holding his head down low as bullets tore into the concrete above him, chunks of mortar exploding and flying around his head. He got to Dub, took a quick look at the man's side, then shot his head up over the side for a moment. He got to his feet and pulled the cameraman's beefy arm over his shoulder.

Dub screamed in pain, "Oh! Jesus Christ!"

"Ignore it! "Ignore it! We gotta go," Ransom screamed into his ear as they took off running.

The SWAT guys continued firing into the building, strategically picking out gunmen and directing the fire towards them. The men inside ran for cover, several of them falling to the ground with muffled cries of pain. Then the shooting stopped, as the gunmen inside pulled the hostages to their feet, headed out of the rotunda, and disappeared from sight.

Dub and Brick stumbled past the corner of the hospital wing. After stealing a fleeting glance over his shoulder, Brick left Dub lying behind the cover of the building and ran over to where Sam Ballard and his men were huddled.

"I need an ambulance over here! I need an ambulance!"

Sam nodded at him, and a group of his men ran over to Dub.

Phelps stepped forward. "Good plan, Ransom. Excellent work."

Ransom hesitated, then turned and headed back to where the injured cameraman was lying.

***

The noise was deafening and came without warning.

Nick had been sitting on the floor, still in the darkness, holding his knees against his chest. What the hell was he supposed to do now?

He weighed the options in his mind; they were few and far between.

Best-case scenario, he snuck down the corridor, found another way out of the building, and made his escape completely undetected. Next case, he waited in the building for the FBI or the SWAT team to raid the building, scavenge the corridors, and rescue his cowering ass. The alternate version of that scenario was that he waited, and he waited, before the FBI decided it was a no-win situation, and either the gunmen found him, or they took a bomb and blew the place sky high, with him in it. That was, by no means, a best-case scenario.

Then there were the worst-case scenarios. He waited, and he hid, only to be found, and turned into a hostage himself, another chip on the bargaining table. Or worst of all, he snuck out of this room, tried to make a run for it, and was either shot and killed, or was tortured, and then shot and killed.

Each was a sunshiny option, but the worst was waiting in the room, wondering if he would be rescued. Whether he would live or die. He had no idea how to carry out an escape, but he was starting to see the coward's death as an inevitability, while the hero's death was a fifty-fifty gamble. After pushing his luck with Morgan for the better part of a year, he was getting more comfortable with splitting the difference.

He walked over to the door, pressed his weight against the wooden face, and turned the handle ever so slowly. The latch pulled silently from its metal pocket in the doorframe, and clicked into place at the end of its rotation. Nick took a slow breath, held it, and started pulling the door towards himself as he pressed his left hand against the wooden frame. He peered out into the empty corridor, and was just about to sweep the door the rest of the way open, when a sharp cracking noise echoed through the building. It was followed by a thundering volley of quick, staccato gunfire, and then the ricocheting sounds of shattering glass. He nearly slammed the door shut in his panic, but caught himself, and slowly pressed it closed.

He could hear himself breathing.

"Fuck," he thought. "Fuck. Fuck. Fuck. Fuck. Fuck."

The gunfire continued. He closed his eyes. Better to know what was happening than sit in this room like a caged dog. He again opened the door, paused, and stepped out into the short, darkened hallway that led out to the corridor. He legs grew stiff with each explosion of glass. He could hear people screaming in terror. Then came the yelling. Someone had been hit. A man. One of the attackers.

Nick clenched his hands, gritted his teeth, and walked to the end of the hall, his arms and legs loose. If he got shot, he got fucking shot. He peered around the corner just as things started happening.

Two men were walking past the end of the hall. They

appeared to be in no hurry. Their body language was angry, but not panicked. They were followed a moment later by a third man, who seemed more on the defensive, like his duty was to guard his comrades. This man held his gun at attention, and glanced behind him as he hurried away. Then the tide started moving. Another gunman, this one cursing and yelling, came down the hall. He was followed by about a half dozen civilians - students, nurses, and cafeteria workers - who jumped or held their hands to their heads every time shots were heard.

"Shut the fuck up!" one of the men yelled. "Keep moving!"

Two more gunmen walked past the end of the hallway. Then another half dozen hostages followed behind. One of the men glanced down the hall as he went by. Nick pulled his head back.

Goddammit. Had he seen him?

Nick waited.

Then the rushing of feet. Clamoring.

"Leave them!" one of the men yelled.

More men came rushing past. They were yelling to each other.

Then something big went off.

BoOoOoooom!

The lights flickered, and the floor shook. A bomb? The sound rumbled the air. Nick threw his hands to his head instinctively, as though he'd been hit. The first boom was followed by the sounds of twisting metal and crumbling concrete, which continued for several moments, then slowly stopped.

Nick leaned his head towards the corner again, sliding one eye past the edge of the wall until he had a clear view. The air was filled with dust and smoke. Two more men ran past, the last one stopping to look behind him. Then the sounds of heavy fire doors being closed, and a solid *kajunking* noise as something was slammed against metal.

"Is that thing secure? Check it," the guy yelled.

His comrade grunted back at him. "It's good."

Then the second man rushed past, and the two of them were gone.

The gunfire had stopped. The sounds of the people leaving the area died down.

What had happened?

How did it stand now?

Nick waited to see if any of the men would be coming back.

All he could hear were the sounds of sizzling wires. Then somewhere, far off in the building, a fire alarm started going off. But there was no sound of anyone returning.

He was just about to run down the hall to investigate, when the phone in the next room starting ringing. He ran inside, caught it at the start of the next ring, and clasped the handset in his hands. He waited. Listened to see if the phone had drawn attention.

Nothing.

His hands were sweating.

He raised the receiver to his ear, took a breath, and whispered, "Hello?"

***

They brought the new group of hostages in. From the looks of them, they were mostly students and lab workers. Jeff watched as they were led into the lab and directed towards the back of the room, where he and the rest of the group sat on the floor, their backs against the wall, literally and figuratively. Jesus. It didn't look like any of them had been injured, but that didn't mean there weren't dead or dying people around the building. They'd probably just been left upstairs. After the commotion they'd heard just a few moments ago, Jeff and the rest of the group, Renoir, Nina, David, and Raj, were certain that the cavalry had arrived. Unfortunately, the job wasn't finished. Tim and his men were losing ground, getting pushed back inside the hospital, which meant their options would only be getting more desperate.

"What happens now?" Jeff whispered to Nina.

His friend, advisor, and occasional flame, Nina Parker was known in the business world for her unshakeable calm. At the Foundation, her unflappable, detached reasoning on nearly every business matter had earned her an icy, merciless reputation, mostly because her determinations usually led her to reorganize and regroup, which meant people were let go. Jeff never liked to do that, which was why he left that part of the management to his leadership team, but he had to admit, when Nina made a decision, it usually straightened things out, and quickly. She was a skilled surgeon, scanning the body, looking for the problems, and removing them piece by piece with infinite precision. Still, that wasn't necessarily an endearing quality.

Nina cleared her throat. Her eyes scanned the room calmly.

"Whatever just happened upstairs, our friend with the gun came out one notch down."

Jeff waited for her to continue.

"I can't imagine that their original plan involved them holing up in the basement of the building. They've gotta be looking for a new way out. That can only mean..." She trailed off.

"That can only mean what?" Jeff asked.

She turned to him.

When she spoke, there was a whispery rasp in her voice, something Jeff had never heard before.

"That can only mean trouble for someone in this room."

No sooner did she say it, than trouble showed its face. Tim and his second in command barked orders to the gunmen scattered around the room, who quickly scattered, hoisted their guns in the air, and screamed at the trapped crowd.

"You move!" they shouted. "Move!"

The crowd, some of whom had slumped over lab counters or sat on stools and chairs around the room, staggered to their feet, weary.

"Back of the room!" the gunmen shouted.

The crowd moved, their arms in the air, eyes nervous, unsure what effect even the slightest hesitation or confusion might have. Once the majority of them had been lined up against the back wall, the gunmen fanned out, one standing at each of the half-dozen doors going in and out of the lab. Three stood in the middle of the room, guns raised, scanning the crowd. A tenth man walked over to Tim and whispered something in his ear.

Tim nodded and walked across the room, between two of the gunmen. Then he said, "Would my original guests please step forward?"

Jeff's heart murmured in his chest. No doubt his companions

were feeling the same sensation. Nina was right. What now?

Tim raised his voice. "Please step forward! We will not be waiting on you."

The five of them stood. Renoir climbed to his feet with a grunt of pain. Nina and David rose, their expressions defiant. Raj sort of shuffled forward, hand still clasped to wrist. They all stepped forward, emerging from the crowd, ghosts through the trees.

"Thank you. Now, would the bunch of you be so kind as to make your way into the back room please."

Tim nodded towards the glassed-in room. Jeff's jaw dropped. *Oh my God.*

"Its not what you think," Tim cooed. "It's not what you think. You're of no use to me dead, people."

They were all rocking their weight on the balls of their feet. This last sentence seemed to give them one last nudge forward, and they began walking. They were almost to the door when Tim spoke again."

"Not you, Mr. Drake."

David stopped in his tracks.

"It is Mr. Drake?" Tim continued. "If this is Jeff Pepper, the two of you can only be Ms. Parker and Mr. Drake. You're his guy and girl Friday, respectively, are you not?"

Nina held Tim in a cold, steady gaze. David stood in the middle of the room, slowly turning towards the man who clearly knew more about him than he wanted to let on.

"Yes, I know who all of you are now," Tim said slowly. "Now, how can the coincidence of *you* being *here,* help *me* get out *there?* Oh, I know."

Tim motioned towards two of his men, who walked over, grabbed David by each of his arms, and headed out of the room.

"David!" Nina shouted.

"What do you want?!" Jeff bellowed. "Tell me what you want and I'll get it for you."

Tim walked over to the far wall, where he gingerly selected one of the white canisters, which he cradled in his hands as he crossed the room. He stopped in front of Jeff and stared him in the face.

"You're gonna get me what I want either way."

"I have a chopper on the roof. The pilot is sitting at the controls, ready to go."

Tim hesitated. "What good would a helicopter do me, Mr. Pepper, if the minute I climb on board, the police shoot me down?"

"We can make sure that they don't."

"How?"

"Tell them I'm on board," Jeff said matter of factly.

Tim again hesitated. "I think the boys out there still need a little lesson. David will help me with that part."

Jeff struggled to control himself. "If anything happens to him-"

Tim looked from Jeff to the canister in his hand. For a moment it looked as if the man might be considering a change in his plans. Then he stepped back, motioned for David and two of the gunmen to exit the room, and walked out behind them.

***

Ransom was talking to Nick, asking him what he could see from inside the building, but so far, the little punk was totally useless.

No kidding some people had been shot. You don't say? Yeah? There were hostages? Fascinating...

This information was nothing new.

Who were these people? How many of them were there? What did they want? That's what they needed to find out.

Brick glanced over at Morgan, who had been ushered away from the crowd and now sat on the sidewalk with her back against the wall, her legs hugged up to her chest. Jesus, she was sexy. What kind of a guy landed a girl like that? Where was the *justice* in this world? This Nick guy didn't sound like any great shakes at the moment. He was certainly no help from the inside. Ransom was just about to start venting his frustrations into the phone, when a hush settled over the crowd around him, and he noticed Phelps was again on the phone, waving his hand in the air for silence. Brick glanced at Murray, who gave him a matter of fact response.

"It's them again."

"Hello, this is Agent Phelps. Who am I speaking with?" He nodded his head slowly. "Okay, Tim, what do you want? We're here to help you."

There was a pause. Phelps pressed his chin into his chest, clearly restraining himself.

"Yes, well, let me assure you, that confrontation a few minutes ago was not under my authority," he glared at Ransom. "We're here to help you. We don't want any more casualties."

Another pause.

Ransom was about ready to crawl out of his skin.

"Yes, we're aware that Mr. Pepper is in the building."

Phelps grew quiet.

"Yes, we know Mr. Drake-"

He stopped short.

"Hello? Tim?" Phelps turned to Murray. "The phone's dead."

"He hung up." Murray responded, "Want me to-"

A gasp went up from the crowd. The agents raised their heads, looking towards the building. There, above the entrance to the rotunda, a lone figure in a business suit was walking out into a glassed-in room.

"Who is that? There's someone there!" a woman shouted.

Ransom looked over at Murray questioningly.

"That's David Drake," Murray replied. "He's one of Jeff Pepper's people."

"What's he got in his hand?" Ransom asked.

Murray raised a pair of binoculars to his eyes. He trained the lenses on the building, racing down the side to the windows, where he found the figure of David Drake, standing alone, his expression ashen, afraid. Murray lowered his gaze to Drake's right hand. He was holding a small white canister, one with a blue metal control panel along the top.

"What is that thing?" Phelps said.

Murray dropped the binoculars. "Beats the hell out of me."

As they stood watching, Drake, his movements jerky and forced, raised the canister to his chest, hesitated, then lifted his left hand to meet it. Murray watched through the binoculars again, focusing on Drake's hands as his fingers worked a switch along the top of the canister. After a moment of fumbling, the switch clicked into place, and a series of blue LED lights flickered along the top.

Ransom turned to Phelps, then looked past him towards several TV news crews that had set up shop along the sidewalk, where they were now filming the action unfolding.

"Phelps, you might want to get these TV people out of here. They could end up getting something no one wants to-"

A shout went up from the crowd.

Ransom looked back to the building as it started-

A whisper of vapor puffed out from the canister and swirled in the air around Drake. For a moment nothing seemed to be happening, then a look of horror and a grimace of pain flashed across David Drake's face, before the man vanished, and a hemorrhaging, rupturing figure took his place. Blood oozed from Drake's eyes and ears. The skin around his face lost all shape, rippling and bulging like a balloon left out in the sun. Then everything, face, features, neck, seemed to pulse and bubble, before every inch of skin, every pore, every human element turned inside out and exploded in a geyser of churning blood and pulp.

Ransom turned away as the bloody silhouette of what had once been David Drake twisted in the misty red air and fell to the floor. Men and women in the crowd were screaming in terror. Ransom heard the sounds of people getting sick. Even the news guys, always the most cynical folks at any crime scene, looked as though they might lose it any second.

"Holy *fucking SHIT!*" a young guy in the back shouted.

"I couldn't have said it better," Phelps muttered to his men.

"Anybody ever seen anything like *that* before?"

They all shook their heads.

"That was something very new," Aftab stammered.

"All right then," Phelps responded. "I'm gonna go out on a limb here and suggest we throw that device into the mix as a possible motive for these guys being here. Anyone have a problem with that?"

No one said a word.

***

What the hell?

The agent he'd been talking with had completely left him hanging.

"Hello?" Nick shouted into the phone. *"HELLOOOO?!"*

Nothing. Asshole.

"HEY! Hello?!!"

Still nothing. Then –

"Keep your fucking voice down, kid!" the voice squawked through the receiver.

"Where were you man?"

"Shit came up," Ransom responded.

"What do I do now?" Nick asked.

"I need you to check on some things for me. Get me some info from inside."

"What do you want me to do?"

***

Go down the hall! That's what he wanted him to do. What kind of agent was this? In a situation like this, weren't they supposed to be making sure the people inside were safe?

Now, here he was, walking the down the hallway, listening for even the slightest sound from any direction. Wondering if someone was gonna jump out and pop him in the head.

The first steps out of the back room were the hardest. The tension in the air seemed to crackle around him, *literally crackle!* The lights were flickering. Something was shorting out. Nick could hear the low, sharp sizzle of fizzling wires. He smelled the smoke of burning insulation. And something else. Gunpowder. The air tasted of metal. He strained his ears, feeling the hairs on his neck standing at attention.

Listening.

Listening.

Nothing.

He got to the end of the corridor and again hesitated. A mirror, cut in the shape of a fruit wedge, was hung across from the intersection of the two corridors. It was placed at an angle where wall and ceiling met, to let people see if someone was about to run them down with a cartful of beakers and Bunsen burners. If Nick was armed, the mirror might make for an even playing field. As it was, if anyone came down that corridor, they'd immediately see his reflection in the mirror, and then, more likely than not, he'd be dead.

He pressed his back against the wall. Eyes locked on the mirror. Heart pounding. Beads of sweat sprung from his temples.

All was clear. No movement.

Nick took a series of quick steps out into the hallway, turned to the right, and ran along the wall. As he reached the end of the next hall, he glanced up at another mirror hung up against the ceiling, and shot around that corner as well. Then he stumbled to a stop. The double doors leading into the rotunda were shut. Nick stepped closer to the doors, his hand reaching for the handles. Then he stopped. A thin silver wire, no thicker than a thread, was wrapped around the handles. Nick leaned closer. The wire did one loop around each handle, then ran across the front of the door, held to the metal with small strips of tape. At the doorframe, the wire turned and ran down to the floor, where it disappeared into a small metal cylinder, no bigger than a pint of milk, that was taped against the wall. There were no flashing lights. No timers or gizmos like you'd see in the movies, but somehow Nick knew what this was.

He stood and headed down another corridor. After a moment he came to another exit from this building. These doors were also rigged up with the same sort of device.

Nick ran down another corridor, and then another.

Both were rigged up with the same contraptions.

He tracked his way back to the first corridor and again picked up the phone.

***

"Shit," Ransom said, covering the mouthpiece on the phone and turning to Phelps. "The doors are wired."

"Wired like how?" Phelps asked, as he twirled one end of his moustache in his fingers.

"Wired like *boom.*"

"Well, that's to be expected," Murray muttered.

Ransom pulled his hand away from the mouthpiece, pacing back and forth as he pontificated. "Listen kid, I'm coming in there."

Phelps narrowed his eyes, shaking his head from side to side jerkily.

"In the meantime, see if you can't find yourself a cell phone somewhere. That'll make all this reconnaissance work just a wee bit easier. Write down this number. Otherwise, I'll be giving you a call again in a few minutes."

Ransom hung up the phone and immediately marched away from Phelps and the flurry of questions he knew would be swirling his way.

He turned to Murray.

"I need you to get me inside. Gimme the best route, and if you say anything about crawling through a heating duct I'm gonna be very skeptical."

"No heating ducts," Murray responded, not missing a beat. "I figured this was coming, so I started going through the plans during your camera guy's little bullet and glass dance routine."

"By the way, get that tape from him and double check the footage of Griffin. I want to make sure its him."

Murray nodded. "I'm way ahead of you. It's him."

Ransom smirked. "You act like you've worked with me before."

"Yeah, wonder what that's all about. Funny thing about Griffin, not only has he killed the hostages at the end of every one of these operations, but he's also taken out almost all the guys working with him on each job."

"And how did he do that? Bombs?"

"You got it," Murray replied.

"All right, what have you got for me? Pull up your little battle plan."

Murray flipped his laptop around and started punching at the keys. "You got it."

"Ransom, lets have a little talk, shall we?" Phelps was now looming over Ransom's shoulder. "Do I need Murray here to pull up a little chart of the chain of command while he's at it?"

Ransom took a deep breath.

Fucking red tape.

Fucking southern bookworm, goody two-shoed, waxed-moustached, and funky-hatted pain in his SWAT-team-spirited, hospital-raiding, hostage-rescuing ass.

"*What,* Phelps? You wanna waste more time? You wanna wait and see who else this guy sets up in a little display room and blows to *kingdom come?*"

"We can't just let loose here," Phelps said. "This isn't some movie, and you're not Bruce Willis."

Ransom bristled. He loved Bruce Willis.

Showtime.

The turning point soliloquy.

"Look, Phelps, I'm not asking to go in there and start shooting out lights while wire-fighting in the air like some sort of kung fu ham bone. I wanna do this carefully, and I wanna do this right, but you just saw what I saw, and the way I figure, this isn't just a hostage situation anymore. We've gotta think about the people inside, but we've also gotta think about what we just witnessed. We can't let him kill anyone else, and we can't let him get away with whatever the hell that stuff was he just used on Jeff Pepper's guy. You wanna stay out here and negotiate, talk into a phone with some guy who doesn't want to take the call? Maybe pussyfoot around here and see if you can talk him into letting one or two folks go? Talk about cars and planes and taking them to the runway, all that nonsense. I think you and I both know this guy's not gonna go for that. If anything, he's gonna get out of there somehow, probably without us knowing, and leave behind a little bomb to blow the place sky high as soon as he's a block or two away."

"You're probably right, but-"

"But what? Gimme three of these SWAT guys, let Murray here gimme a little triptic itinerary, and send me on my way. What do ya say?"

Ransom looked at Phelps, who looked at Murray, who stood expectantly, his fingers on the edge of the monitor.

"What have ya got for him, Murray?" Phelps muttered.

***

It was Ransom and two other guys. Gomez and Lucifer. Brick had worked with both men before.

The guys back at headquarters, the ones who'd thought up the "Agent Butterfingers" title, were always quick to test out nicknames on the newcomers. When Lucifer first joined up two years ago, they'd tried to nickname him "Lucy." When they saw the way he handled a gun, they quickly changed it to "Luke."

Where Luke was serious, and above all things, humorless about his name, Gomez was the jokester, more than adept at his job, but never overwhelmed by the situations their line of work got them into. He also had a penchant for eating marshmallow circus peanuts, and kept the pockets of his vest and cargo pants stuffed with them.

They took the elevator to the top of the north wing, where it was just a one story climb to the roof. The smoke from the construction site fire was thick in the air as they opened the hatch and stepped out onto the gravel and tar roof.

"Christ, man! It stinks out here," Gomez said.

Ransom pulled out the field printouts of Murray's plans - both an overhead view and a series of smaller pages with cross sections of the buildings. Since the hospital and the medical center had been built in sections over the past 70 years, each building was both a snapshot of the architectural tastes of its particular decade and an illustration of the financial and service needs as perceived by the university's board of directors at the time of construction. As a result, every building was a three-dimensional, very tangible economic bar column. In short, none of the rooftops were the same level, which meant getting from one end of the hospital to the other was going to be a bitch, but with the inside route rigged up like a dirty bomb version of *Mouse Trap*, this was the only way to get into the guts of the Health Sciences Building and start cutting out the bad guys.

"How the hell are we supposed to get from here to over there?" Gomez asked, pointing a finger to the far end of the complex.

"Lots of jumping onto hard concrete. Some leaping over chasms," Ransom replied.

"Sounds like fun," Luke said.

The first connection between wings wasn't that bad, maybe

an eight foot drop from one roof to the next. Luke uncoiled a thin roll of black wire and fished it through the end of a small, slick grappling hook. He wrapped the rig around his chest, twisting the ends of the hook under the cable to the side of his right hip.

"Might as well get started," he growled.

Then, without another word, he turned, flexed his legs, one knee cracking audibly, and took off running. At the edge of the roof he tucked into a squat, sprang up into the air, and leapt onto the next roof, where he landed with a muffled thud, stumbling and falling to his knees, then quickly jumping back to his feet.

Gomez turned to Ransom, flashing him a look of comical panic.

"Oh man, at least my girl likes tending to my wounds. This is gonna hurt."

Ransom nodded, trying to hide his fear. Then the two of them ran for the edge of the roof, hurled themselves up into the air, and glanced down over the edge of the building at the crowd down below. For a moment they seemed to hover in the air. Then they crashed down, a Tasmanian Devil cloud of tumbling equipment and flailing limbs. The two of them climbed back to their feet, picked off the pieces of roofing and bird crap, and took off running to catch up with Luke.

NEGOTIATIONS

They moved the group into the glassed-in room in the back of the lab. For some reason the change of location made Raj especially mouse-like. His left hand was constantly creeping to the back of his neck, where it scratched up to his scalp before suddenly dropping down and clasping his right hand. Jeff watched this display a half-dozen times until he finally spoke up.

"What the hell are you doing, Gupta? Why are you so nervous?"

Raj didn't say anything, but swallowed visibly.

"For Christ's sake, just say something!" Jeff yelled.

"This is the staging area." Raj said.

"Staging area?" Nina asked.

"For the project," Gupta answered. "This is the room where we tested the formula on the animals."

Jeff took a deep breath. "And I'm sure we're not talking flea and tick formula, right?"

"No," Raj said calmly. "And before you ask, we're not talking about a cure for that virus, either. That never worked out. The research pinwheeled off in a different direction, something very much outside my field."

Jeff stared at him. His mouth tightened.

Raj continued, "It was more of a... weapon. If put into the right hands. It could just as easily be used to wipe out carriers of the infection. Instead of hoping the virus would burn itself out, thereby bringing about its own demise, this would act to speed things along."

"The whole God thing," Jeff said.

"Maybe," Gupta nodded. "Certainly in the wrong hands I'd say that might be a possibility."

"An inevitability," Renoir muttered.

Nina looked up. "So that canister?"

"That's it," Raj whispered. "Most likely, your friend is dead."

Nina and Jeff fell silent.

The people scattered around the edges of the room were whispering to one another or crying softly. Others sat and stared, mentally removing themselves from their current situation.

"If we get out of here. *When* we get out of here," Jeff said in a slow, deliberate voice. "Your career is over. I'll do everything in my power to be sure you go to jail for this."

"That's the least of my concerns now," Raj replied.

"So how does it work?" Renoir asked. His voice was growing weaker as time went on.

Jeff looked at the older man. In the hour or so that he'd seen him, Renoir's face and hands had turned about ten shades lighter. His face was glazed with a mist of cold sweat. His lips were pale. The blood loss was taking its toll.

"The formula is delivered in a gaseous state. It acts on

contact, whether inhaled through the lungs or transferred to the nervous system through physical contact with the skin. Within a few moments of exposure, cells, every cell, almost instantaneously deteriorates and breaks down."

"And I'm sure that's not pretty," Jeff muttered.

Raj shook his head. "But it acts too quickly for the subject to feel any pain."

"I'm sure you'd like to believe that," Jeff continued. "Makes it easier on you."

"Not that that's a consideration," Renoir added. "He's never exactly been the most humane researcher in our department."

"In what range does this concoction of yours take effect?" Nina interrupted.

Raj looked away from the men, turned to Nina and responded in a slightly condescending tone. "If it's in the air in a self-contained environment, like this room, the range is virtually unlimited. Larger areas may bring partial exposure, but the effects are still lethal. The question of a safe distance is virtually irrelevant."

"So, I'll just say what you're worrying about. What we're all worrying about then," Jeff said. "You think they're gonna kill us."

Raj said nothing.

"Any idea what we can do about it?" Jeff asked.

Raj glanced through the glass at the gunmen in the next room, then turned and looked towards the hostages lined up against the back wall. Satisfied that no one else was watching, he reached down to a drawer near the bottom of the lab bench and slowly pulled it open. Two metal canisters rolled from the back of the drawer forward, clinking against one another as they rolled to a stop.

***

Ransom was hurting by the time they reached the west wing of the hospital.

This was something new.

Time was, he could run across three football field-length rooftops, jump down from any number of gravel-covered rooftops, climb up just as many brick walls and AC systems, and still not break a sweat. Now he was definitely in some pain.

Was it was getting time to start thinking of settling down, maybe take a desk job, squire a serious lady friend, like Victoria, or that chick Morgan? Maybe it was, maybe it was.

Still, the last 10 or 15 minutes had been a lot of fun, and now his adrenaline was pumping to beat the band, so he might hold off on the desk job for now, stick with the exciting work a little bit longer. Victoria and Morgan were another matter. Whichever one got to him first, that was good enough for him. Which reminded him of his onion tartlet; it was after all "seal the deal night," and he still had a lot of prep work to wrap up when this whole situation was resolved. His mouth was watering in anticipation, hot, delicious anticipation. His only hope was that Victoria's performance would live up to that of his tartlet; it would be some tight competition.

"You ready for this?"

"You bet your ass I am," Ransom answered without hesitation, the tip of his tongue tickling the corner of his mouth.

"Uh, don't look at me that way man," Gomez responded. "You're freaking me out."

Ransom snapped to attention. Stop thinking about the tartlet, Ransom!

"I meant I was ready to move in and get this thing done."

"We all clear on the battle plan?" Luke asked.

"Not a bit," Gomez said.

Luke pulled out a printout of Murray's plans and flipped to the second page. "Assuming these guys have rigged all the exterior and adjoining doors, our best bet is to come in through the ventilation housing on the roof-"

"Goddammit!" Ransom muttered.

"What?" Luke asked.

"It's just so clichéd. I was trying to avoid the air ducts; they always do that in the movies. You know that never works."

"We don't go in through the ducts. We just get into the building through the exhaust fans for the ventilation system, then we pop out a panel on the inside and go through the maintenance accesses above the top floor."

"And how do we get down to where these guys are standing, rubbing their hands together and cackling?" Gomez asked.

Luke ran his hand over to a cross-section diagram of the building. He stopped on a glass-enclosed stairwell at the southeast corner. "To get downstairs we're gonna take the express route, open the hatch above the back stairs, hitch a rig to the cross beam, and repel down down the middle of the stairwell as quickly as possible without cracking our heads on the handrails."

"Then what?"

"Then we find this kid and see if he can show us around." Ransom answered.

The three of them looked at the plans one more time, then exchanged glances.

Ransom nodded his head. "Let's do it."

Luke pulled out a Zippo-sized gadget, flipped open the top, and exposed a small, two pronged metal fork, which he lifted to one corner of the ventilation housing and fit into a matching set of eyes on the top of one of the fastening bolts. He pressed his thumb against the back of the tool, and a tiny motor quickly spun the fork around, twirling the bolt free in seconds. He did this for each of the remaining bolts and tipped the cover free. Gomez and Ransom helped him lower it silently to the rooftop. With the cover free, the hot air from the exhaust system began swirling around them. Ransom looked in through the metal screens and saw two massive fan blades whirling about inside.

"What do we do about those?" he began, but was cut short as Luke pulled open the breaker panel on the side of the exposed ducting, studied the inside fleetingly, and jammed another fork-shaped tool between two circuits, which immediately shorted out the system, sending up a plume of smoke.

"How many of those fork things have you got?" Ransom asked.

"Plenty," Luke replied as he pulled the cover from the fan, moved the blade to the side with his foot, and leaned his back against the metal ducting. "See you inside." He pulled his arms against his chest and slid into the darkness.

Ransom and Gomez listened carefully for a thump or a muffled scream.

Gomez looked at Ransom a little warily. This was the part of the operation where Brick was often known to get a case of the… butterfingers, or at least, that was the rumor. Gomez knew the guy's reputation in the department, and especially in this type of operation, was top notch, but there was a part of him that couldn't help but worry about getting tripped up if the guy had one of his Inspector Clouseau incidents in the middle of the job. Oh hell, what was he worrying about? Luke was the one who would probably end up running into trouble. He was humorless, and he was mechanical, and at this moment, God only knew where he was slipping and sliding to inside the building ventilation system. After a few moments, when no sounds of panic or stifled agony echoed up to them from the access hatch, Gomez and Ransom each climbed up to the entrance of the system and followed Luke's example.

***

Phelps was on the phone now, trying to get an answer from inside the building. Tim hadn't answered the phone on the last three attempts. This did not bode well for the chances of negotiation. He hung up, dialed again, and waited. The phone rang five times, started to click into the lab's voicemail account, then, just as Phelps was about to hang up, a voice came on the line.

"Are you trying to sweat us out?"

"Excuse me?" Phelps asked.

"Agent Phelps," Tim responded. "The ventilation inside the building has been turned off. Are you aware of this? I have a hard time believing that you aren't."

"There could be a million reasons for that." Phelps responded. He was trying to sound in control. "As you know, there was a pretty good sized fire at the construction site next door. And in case you've forgotten, the front of the building just got chewed up pretty good with gunfire. More likely than not, something's shorted out or gotten nicked."

There was silence on the other end of the line.

"Are you still with me?" Phelps continued. "I think we have more important things to discuss than the status of your air conditioning, don't we? I'd like to know a bit of the objective behind this whole operation of yours. What'll it take to get you to let some hostages out of there?"

"There won't *be* any hostages coming out of here."

Phelps stopped cold.

He'd dealt with guys like this before. In most cases it was just talk, swagger. A few comments about what they were doing there, what they wanted, and then they'd let something slip, something telling, the name of their home country, or a mention of their family, something, anything that would let Phelps get a little knife blade in there, so he could work and jiggle the blade, pull back the cover and get inside the workings of the big machine. These guys all had a purpose in their heads, cracked or otherwise, something that made them think they had a right, an obligation, to do whatever the hell they wanted, just so long as it was all in the pursuit of their "mission."

Only this guy was different. He didn't seem to have the need to talk, which led Phelps to believe that he wasn't planning to use the people inside the building as pawns. More likely than not, the folks he had squirreled away in that building were more of a hassle to him than a negotiating chip, and if Murray was right about Griffin's past operations, those people were in some serious danger.

"What do you mean 'there won't be any hostages coming out of there?'"

"I'm not interested in these people, or in trading their lives for mine. You're going to let me out of this building, Agent Phelps. You're going to provide me with transportation out of here. And then you'll find these people inside the building, safe and sound."

"I'd like to see that happen, but I'll need some sort of good-faith gesture on your part," Phelps said slowly.

"Good faith," Tim laughed. "Ohh, Agent Phelps-"

Then there was silence again. Jesus, what the hell did *that* mean? What a goddamn annoying laugh! What in the bloody hell was this guy here for?

Phelps flashed on the image of that guy Drake going up in a cloud of pink mist. Whatever the hell was in the canister, *that* was what Ted, or *Griffin* rather, was here for. He was just out on the town, picking up new and exotic weapons. Nabbing a few essentials with a five-finger discount, and all he wanted to do was get out with minimal hassle. But what happened with shoplifters when they got caught? They either gave up, ran, or put up a fight. This guy was definitely gonna put up a fight, unless Phelps found a way to make him happy.

"Look, let's talk. What kind of transportation do you need? How many people are we talking about here? How many men do you have with you?"

That's when Griffin said something that really made Phelps worry.

"One. I only need transportation for one."

***

Everyone tried to read the expression on his face as he hung up the phone, but it was no go. By now they were sure law enforcement was in communication with the group, but it didn't seem like any headway was being made.

"You know they were rigging up the doors with something as we were leaving, right?" one of the women in the back the room whispered.

"We're not getting out of here," another replied.

Jeff seemed to be mulling something in his head. If anyone could do something to convince this guy, or buy him off, it would probably be him. It would have to be. Thats what he was asking himself anyways.

Could money buy your way out of trouble?

Sometimes.

Course, it didn't work for Martha.

It sort of worked for those White House buddies though. Bastards.

But this wasn't anything like that. These guys were terrorists, or at the minimum, militant whack jobs. Their idea of reasoning was blowing something up, or shooting someone in the back of the head when they got too vocal. So far the group had been lucky.

The bleeding in Renoir's leg might have stopped. The pant

leg, which had stopped seeping blood, was drying into a caked, blackish mass of fabric. The older man *smelled* of blood now, a mix of iron and humid breath that was enough to curdle your stomach. He had stopped sweating. The cold chills still quivered through his body every few moments, but maybe he had stabilized. Then again, maybe he was slipping into shock.

"I've got to use the facilities," Renoir said suddenly.

"Good luck with that," Someone muttered from the crowd.

Jeff turned and scowled. "Knock it off," he said.

Renoir lurched to his feet and hobbled to the window, where he rapped his fingers on the glass.

"I've got to use the facilities!" he said louder.

One of the men walked over. He motioned with his gun towards the back of the room.

Renoir shook his head angrily.

"The fuck I will!" he boomed.

Renoir started pounding on the glass.

Hard.

His right hand was balled up in a fist, moving back and forth in a disjointed, mechanical motion. His left hand seemed to fall limp at his side.

Jeff looked closer.

No, the left hand was clenching something against Renoir's leg, pressing it against the place that had been bleeding.

"Renoir," he whispered. "What are you trying to *do?*"

Michel's eyes rolled in Jeff's direction, then he spun back to the window, and pounded on the glass still harder, until Tim himself turned and marched into the room, stopping on the other side of the glass.

Renoir stopped knocking and stared at the man.

Tim hesitated, then motioned to the man beside him, who nodded his head and walked over to the entrance of the testing room and opened the door.

"Come on, lets go," the man shouted at Renoir.

"Thank you," the older man replied. He ran the fingers of his right hand through his sweaty hair, took a deep breath, and limped towards the door.

"Be careful," Jeff said as he passed by.

Renoir sighed softly and left the room.

The guard closed the testing room door behind them, and the group watched through the glass as Renoir walked towards the lab exit.

A wave of tension hit the room.

Jeff felt nauseous. This was not going to end well. Whatever was happening, it was not going to end well.

Tim nodded his head towards the door, barking an order to the man with the gun, who nodded in agreement.

Renoir stared straight ahead of him as he limped on his injured leg.

That's when it happened.

Nothing showy.

No sudden movements.

Jeff wasn't even sure how it went down. He was watching one moment, and in the next, in a blink, Renoir had pulled something from his pocket, held it in his bloodstained hands, and pressed a switch on top.

A blue light winked on.

It was one of the canisters.

Tim had turned his head away.

The guard was oblivious as he reached for the doorknob.

Renoir scanned the room, then crouched to the ground, reached out his arm, and rolled the canister along the concrete floor towards Tim's feet.

The metal housing must have made a noise when it hit the ground. As the canister rolled within six feet of Tim, he spun around, and in one swift movement, pulled a gun from his side, crouched to one knee, and shot a single bullet straight into Renoir's forehead. Then he reached out, picked up the canister, and reset the switch.

The blue light went out.

Renoir's arms and legs went slack as he crumpled to the ground and lay still.

Jeff turned away as two of Tim's men walked over, grabbed each of Renoir's arms, and dragged his body out of the room.

Tim got to his feet, shaking his head from side to side in disbelief. Jeff watched Tim's hands closely as he ran them up and down the sides of the canister, then reached behind his back, and tucked the monstrous little weapon into a pocket on the back of his coat.

Simon walked over to the entrance to the testing room and flipped a switch on the wall. The power lock on the metal door clanged shut.

***

So far so good.

He hadn't seriously disabled himself or anyone else yet.

His worst injury was a jammed index finger on his left hand, and that wasn't his trigger finger, so he was good. Luke and Gomez hadn't even seen it happen, which was also good. No need to raise concerns on their part. It wasn't like the same thing couldn't happen to anyone. Hell, they'd just finished rappelling down through the center of a nine-story stairwell, and it hadn't exactly been a clean drop! It was one of those setups where the space between the railings on either side was only about two feet apart - if that - arranged to discourage suicide attempts probably, maybe accidents, but most likely aimed at quashing the self-snuffing tendencies of students, particularly foreign students in the science programs, who were known to crack under the pressure of maintaining a 4.0 GPA in the study of mollusk formulations and the extraction of what, clam juice, for the betterment of society, dental health, and enamel durability. Something ridiculous like that. Who the hell would kill themselves over failed clam juice-extraction? That's what Brick was thinking to himself as he sailed down the center of the shaft, swinging ever so slightly from one side to the other, left to right, dodging the metal railings as he whispered down to the floor.

Course, then another thought had flashed into his head, the thought of that girl Morgan, the drop-dead knock out who was dating that kid inside.

Brick got an image of Morgan's legs as she sat on the stoop outside, waiting for news on her beau.

Her beau.

Jesus! This jackass better be one smooth daddy-o, cause there are few people on earth worthy of a roll in the hay with a girl the likes of that Morgan chicky.

That was Ransom's first mistake -- wistful thoughts of college sirens. One reminiscence of those sweet, perfect, supple legs, and he'd forgotten all about what he was doing at the moment -- rappelling down nine stories in a two foot clearance area, between countless,undoubtedly merciless metal safety bars -- a feet which unfortunately required a bit of focus. He swung out just a bit too far as he got to the bottom, so much so that he didn't quite make it back to the center of the shaft as he approached the first floor, and his hand paid the price. He twisted his body, trying to shift direction, but had only gotten about halfway through the corkscrew before he put out his left hand, and the force of his plummeting body did its best to drive flesh and bone through paint and steel. The flesh and bone was his finger, which got tweaked sharply to the side and in.

Holy shit!

Brick did his best to swallow the resulting scream of pain as he landed on the first floor and shuffled back and out of the way as Luke and Gomez came swooping in behind him.

Neither of them hit their hands on anything.

Goddammit.

Luke flipped open the printout of the building layout, looked around to get his bearings, then gave Brick a quick chin nod, and started for a side corridor. Gomez followed suit, the two of them pulling out their handguns as they approached the doorway. Brick massaged his left hand with his right, then reached over to his side and slipped his own gun from its holster. At least his shooting hand was all right.

Stop! He thought to himself. He needed to stay focused!

"Fuck it," Ransom muttered.

Gomez turned to him questioningly.

"Let's get in there and get this done."

Gomez nodded, then leaned back and kicked open the door.

***

You *motherfuckers,* Jeff thought to himself.

You miserable *sons of bitches.*

The world was filled with decent folks, just trying to get through their days, dealing with asshole bosses, impossible odds, and crooked governments, each hell bent on finagling them into work while fleecing them of their money and leaving them with only a few dollars for hooch and cable.

Why then did the big man upstairs feel it necessary to sprinkle around a handful of truly evil bastards to make things that much worse?

Maybe it wasn't the man upstairs, maybe it was the other guy, if you bought into all that. The whole battle of the fates, struggle between good and evil. Now Jeff had seen a clear display of the evil. The rotten, miserable scum of the earth. He was willing to bet good odds that roughly of a quarter of the world's shitheads were gathered in this room, and no, he didn't mean researchers and medicinal chemists, though that would make for a good line. He meant Tim and Simon and their other miscreant fuckhead accomplices.

There was a pool of drying blood in the center of the room, with a streak of red, like a brushstroke, pulling away from the pool and making an almost graceful arc towards the doorway.

That was the way they'd dragged Michel Renoir's body from the room. Just like that, in a flash, the old man was here, and then he was gone. All he'd ever said, all he'd ever done, the years in school, playing as a child, raising his own family, the talks with his grandchildren at the dining room table, talcum powder, shaving cream, the smell of aftershave. All that stuff. Everything that somehow collectively made a *man*, all of that had just been shot in the face for attempting a noble act of heroism. And now, where was that man? Pulled into a back corner, his still warm body trickling blood.

"Motherfuckers,"

Jeff looked at Tim, and felt his own blood shiver with resignation. Time for payback. Time to start turning the screws.

"Something bothering you, Mr. Pepper?" Tim asked suddenly.

Jeff stared at the man coldly. "What is this all about? Are you ever going to tell me that?"

"There's no big ideal behind it. Not really."

"Then why do it?"

Tim glanced at his watch. "Because someone needs to, and if I don't step in and run this operation *my* way, then someone else will come in and do it the *wrong* way."

"So, you're just a guy out there doing whatever it takes for a paycheck?"

"Up to a point," Tim responded.

"What point?!" Jeff spat. "You're a goddamn terrorist."

Tim shook his head as though pained by such a simple label.

"Look," Jeff was feeling shaky. "I have money. I have *a lot of fucking money*. How much will it take to get us out of here?"

"You and I both know that no amount of money is getting me or any of my men out of here. You can sign a check, or wire us a payment, but if we want to get out of this building, we're going to have to deal with the people outside who don't want us to leave."

"Then let me talk to them. I can get them to listen. I told you, I have a chopper on the roof, we can leave from there. If they know that I'm on board, they'll let you take off, no question."

"But how do I know they'll let us land?"

Jeff's upper lip curled. "Don't you watch the news? I'm the third-richest man in the world, the second wealthiest voter in the United States; that's clout the government doesn't mess with. If I say I need a tax cut, or I mention a way that sneaking illegal workers into the country could help the economy, I get my way. No questions asked. They'll certainly listen if I make some demands about where my personal helicopter sets down."

"I don't want you on board. I go alone."

"Then I can't help you. My pilot only flies when I'm aboard. If he doesn't see me there, he won't go."

"Then I go anyway- he'll hand over the controls."

"Yeah, and the military will shoot you down. Simple as that."

A moment of pissed-off, angry deliberation.

"And what do you want in return?" Tim's voice was growing quieter.

"You've gotta let these people go."

Tim cleared his throat, then nodded his head. "What do we need to do?"

"I'll have to speak to the folks you've been chatting up

outside. Make sure my pilot is at the controls and they won't
swat our little puddle jumper out of the sky."

Tim pulled the handset from its cradle on the wall and
handed it to Jeff. "Make the call."

***

Where were they?

It had been too long since they'd told him they were
coming in, and Nick was starting to get that creeping feeling
in his stomach again. There hadn't been anymore gunfire or
explosions. No more voices down the corridor. No more muffled
exchanges between armed men in the halls. Just the sounds of a
building where all was not right. The smell of burning wire hung
in the air. Occasionally, he could hear a door somewhere in the
building being kicked open or slammed shut, and he could tell
from the directions of these noises that the people who'd taken
over the building had moved everyone to the basement, down
to Raj's labs.

Wow. He'd taken this job for all the right reasons, or
maybe the wrong ones: Medical, dental, steady pay, a decent
work environment, and here he was, holed up in a basement,
armed killers on the loose, breathing in smoke from a scorched
building. He might as well have gone to L.A. and tried his hand
on the misery of a film set, or enlisted in the army. He was
pretty close to getting killed, he was certain about that now.

At least *someone* out there was probably thinking about him.
"Morgan."

The name hovered in the air before him, then the sounds of

shuffling feet outside the door caught his attention. Nick ducked back against the wall, holding his breath. "Jesus."

Someone outside the door was whispering something. Nick heard a hand take hold of the doorknob on the other side. The door swung open slowly as the end of a gun barrel crept through the crack. Then it swung open all the way, and three men entered the room. The one in the lead lunged forward, weapon at the ready.

"You Nick?"

"Yeah."

"Brick Ransom."

Brick shot out his hand for Nick to shake it. His grip was quick and hard.

"We're gonna need your help on this part. Let's get going. You know how to use one of these?" Ransom reached around his waist, pulling a handgun from a pocket on his lower back.

"No."

"It's pretty simple, you've seen the movies. Point, squeeze the trigger, and shoot. Don't let the little fucker jump out of your hands."

Nick nodded and took the gun.

Ransom watched him warily. "You know, just for safety's sake, keep that thing tucked away unless I tell you to use it."

Nick slipped the gun into the pocket on his cargo pants.

Brick motioned towards his team members. "These guys are agents-" he faltered. "Hell, they go by Luke and Gomez."

"What's up, kid?" Gomez nodded.

Luke shot Ransom a look.

"All right, enough chit chat," Ransom continued. "We

better get going. Any idea where they've taken everybody?"

"My guess is downstairs, Raj Gupta's lab."

"Can you take us there?" Luke asked him.

Nick stammered. "Oh, I uh, thought we were leaving."

Ransom shook his head. "Not yet."

Nick swallowed. "Okay then, yeah, I can get you there."

Ransom stepped back and let Nick lead the way out into the corridor. The lights down the length of the hall had begun to flicker.

"Power's fucking up," Gomez said.

"Not surprised," Luke responded.

The four of them hurried through the hall, with Ransom stepping up the pace and walking alongside Nick. At the end of the corridor, they reached a doorway that was propped open. Brick held up his hand for the group to stop, then lifted his gun in his right hand, pressed his back against the wall, and reached out to the door with his left. A twist of his elbow and the door swung open. Ransom lunged around the corner, sweeping his firearm around the stairwell.

Gomez leaned forward, whispering in Nick's ear, "Keep an eye on where he's pointing that thing kid, he's been known to have some accidents."

Nick's eyes darted to the side. He nodded. The group followed behind Ransom as he made his way down the concrete steps.

***

Phelps picked up the phone as his eyes scanned the building. "Ransom, you there?"

"Brick Ransom?" a voice from the handset asked him.

Phelps turned his attention to the voice. "Who is this?"

"This is Jeff Pepper," the voice responded. "I'm calling you from inside the building."

"Mr. Pepper, we were afraid you might be in there-"

"Let me be quick about this," Jeff interrupted him. "I need to know if my pilot is still on the roof."

"That I'm not sure of, Mr. Pepper."

"Then find out. If he *isn't,* then make sure he gets there. I'm going to be leaving the building in the next 10 minutes, and I need my pilot to be waiting for me when I get to the roof."

"Is it just you we'll be looking for?" Phelps asked.

"No. I'll be leaving with a couple of the men from inside, and I'll need your assurance that they'll be allowed to leave safely alongside me."

What was this all about?

Pepper had to be making this call under orders.

Phelps watched Murray's expression. The other agent looked at him closely.

"Of course, we'll let you all take off without incident," Phelps replied. "And Mr. Pepper-"

"Yes," Jeff asked expectantly.

"Is everything all right? Are you okay?"

"I'm fine," the voice responded. " Just make sure Michael is on the roof when we get there-"

The line went dead. Phelps turned to Murray.

"You still know how to fly?"

Murray blinked. "I haven't been at the controls in years, but it should come back to me."

Good, cause Pepper's requesting that his helicopter pilot meet him upstairs, and there's no way I'm letting these guys use that guy to get out of here scott free.

"Just get me a uniform and send me up there."

***

"We'll be heading upstairs shortly with Mr. Pepper."

Tim was standing in the corner addressing Jason, Simon's right-hand man. He was still holding the phone receiver, twirling the ragged phone wires from when he'd pulled it from the wall at the end of Jeff's call.

"As soon as we're airborne, I'll radio down and tell you what we've worked out," Tim continued.

"And what will *that* be?" Jason asked.

Tim's eyes narrowed. "Don't you trust me?"

"Just want to know what to expect."

Simon stepped forward, putting himself between Jason and Tim. "We'll tell you when it's final."

Jason hesitated, "That's fine."

Tim reached towards Jason, pulled a gun from the man's side holster, looked him in the eyes, then walked away. Simon clenched a hand around Jeff's elbow and pulled him out of the room. They stepped out into the hall as the doors slammed shut behind them. As they walked away, Jeff caught a glimpse of Nina's face, staring after him, her mouth set at a very unusual angle. She was worried.

***

They were at the top of the glass-enclosed stairwell on the building's south side when they heard someone coming, actually, several people coming. The footsteps were muffled, the voices hushed, to the point that Ransom damn near kept on going. Then one of the men coughed and Brick's eyes shot open. The four of them rushed back up the stairs and slipped out of the stairwell on the first floor, where they prayed the oncoming group would continue upstairs.

Ransom leaned his head against his shoulder, squeezed the talk button on his radio, and wheezed into the radio, "We've got movement in the south stairs, can you give me an ID?"

There was a pause, then a voice responded, "Give us two seconds, Brick."

The group waited, and the footsteps came closer. Two of the men were talking, arguing about how many "canisters" they could take on board with them. Then the voices stopped at the door to the first floor. Nick's heart shivered. His three companions tightened their grips on their weapons. The radio on Ransom's shoulder coughed feedback and he quickly held his hand over the speaker. Then the voices moved on, rising and falling with the sound of men carrying something heavy.

The radio crackled to life. "We've got three big fish. Looks like Griffin, his right-hand man, and Jeff Pepper are heading up the stairs. They're carrying some sort of flat or gurney between them. It's loaded down with something, ain't a person."

Ransom turned to the three of them. "Three guesses what

that is." Then he spoke into the radio again, "Metal canisters, right?"

Another pause, "That's our guess. Pepper just called in and requested his pilot."

"Shit. Okay. Over and out."

Brick switched off the radio and turned to his team. Well, his team and Nick. That stupid, lucky little monkey Nick. Morgan was probably counting down the seconds til she saw him again, saw him, and smooched him, and- *bah!*

"We'd better split up on this one. You guys go downstairs, get those people out of here. I'm heading for the roof."

"No backup?" Gomez asked skeptically.

"No backup. You've got a lot of people you've got to evacuate."

"If that's what you think's best," Luke replied.

"Go," Ransom barked as he slipped open the stairwell door and looked up through the flights, then down towards the basement. He motioned downstairs, then mounted the stairs and started climbing, taking them two at a time.

Nick watched Brick go, then glanced over his shoulder at Luke and Gomez and started for the basement.

The temperature rose with each step downward. The air was out.

They were just outside the door to the second basement level when they stopped short. Nick reached for the handle of the first door, but Luke's hand shot out and grabbed his wrist.

"Hold it."

"What."

Luke pointed at the strike plate to the right of the handle, where a thin white wire ran out from between the door and the frame, continued down the wall, and slid back under the door.

"Is that wire always there?"

"No."

"Didn't think so." Luke turned to Gomez. "He's got the place wired, just like the other episodes in his file."

Nick looked at them questioningly.

Gomez scratched at his brow. "The guy we're dealing with isn't too well known for letting his hostages go free. He has a nasty habit of blowing them up as he's making his escape."

"And in this case?" Nick asked.

"In this case, one of his guys inside might come out to check on things, and *boom*. Or, second scenario, we come in to save the day, and end up doing the job for them."

"Either way, it's *boom*?" Nick asked.

Gomez turned to Luke, "Not necessarily. With any luck, Luke here hasn't spent all his free time lately looking at internet porn, and did a little studying on disarming explosive switches."

"Sorry," Luke said. "It was all porn, all the time. Haven't gone over that disarming stuff since I first signed on."

Gomez's face fell. "God damn rookie assho-"

"I'm kidding," Luke interrupted. "Gimme five minutes."

Brick started losing steam as he got to the eighth-floor landing. Christ. How long before this would be done and his onion tartlet evening could get started? That was gonna taste better than ever after this ordeal.

The doors to the roof slammed two floors above him.

How fast were they moving?

If he went out there now, would they see him coming up behind them?

It was a pretty flat stretch of roof between the Health Sciences Building and the wing that connected the research building to the main hospital. A few too many opportunities to take some good clean shots at him. He could call out to Phelps, tell him to put some sharpshooters on the three men upstairs, but he knew that was undoubtedly taking place already. Brick leaned against the wall and pressed his thumb on the receiver on his shoulder.

"Can you see 'em up there?"

A crackle, then silence and a hum.

"Yeah," Phelps' voice came through. "We got 'em. They're tucked in behind the stair access on the roof. *Annnd* there they go, they're taking the scenic route."

Brick could picture the scenic route quite clearly. He'd just been over every sunbaked inch of it 15 minutes ago. They were looking for a way to block any possible shots, not that the feds would be crazy enough to try that with Jeff Pepper in the middle of the situation, but nevertheless he knew the route they'd be taking: Right across the northern most side of the building, where the brick façade rose up about six feet to their left and the ventilation and air equipment closed them in on the right, giving them a little rooftop corridor for some cover. Hell, there was no reason for him to go up to the top and pop out where they could see him. That would be stupidest move he could pull. The smarter route would be to cut through the building on the next floor, circumvent his way into the main wing, and come at them as they neared the helipad.

173

He sucked in a deep breath, lifted his foot, and took off up the stairs in a sprint. Brick darted to the left At the ninth floor, grabbed the handle to the door, and pulled it forward. The air around him hiccupped, them shuddered-

PHHOOM!

The explosion rang in his ears as brick and mortar and plaster tore into his face and neck. He pulled one hand over his eyes as he saw a burst of white, then nothing.

Luke slid the knife blade between the door and the frame, where he held it as close to the wood as possible while pressing a thin strip of metal against the wire. He held the metal steady in his right hand, pulling it down and into place as he lowered his knife, pressed the top of the blade against his leg, and flipped it closed. He tucked the knife into a side pocket, pulled out a roll of silver tape, and tossed it to Nick.

"Tear off a couple of five inch pieces for me, will ya kid?"

Nick spun the tape in his hands, tore off the pieces, and handed them to Luke, who pressed the metal strip against the doorframe until his knuckles turned white, then carefully pressed the tape across the strip and onto the wall, scratching it with his thumbnail to smooth the edges.

The tape held. Luke gave Gomez and Nick a "here goes nothing" eyebrow arch, then turned the handle and pulled the door open. Nothing happened. Luke took the tape and ripped off another strip, which he ran down the inside of the frame, holding the metal strip more securely.

"Was that a lucky guess or what?" he said.

Nick tugged at the back of his shirt, shaking the fabric that clung to his back with sweat.

They started down the corridor.

"What are those?" Nick whispered. He pointed to two rows of white plastic-wrapped bundles that ran down the length of the hall.

"Those," Gomez responded, "are the things we don't want to go off."

Nick nodded and followed behind them as they continued down the hall. They were in the Department of Immunology offices, where he'd spent countless, insufferable hours. Raj filled his weekdays with an endless series of "advisory meetings" with his researchers, during which his impatient, arrogant comments were carried across in his distinctive singsong, whiney lilt. Nick had the distinct displeasure of hearing each and every conversation, as though he too were involved in the meetings. Raj never closed the door to his office, no doubt spooked by stories of abused postdocs of the past who had taken closed-door meetings with their similarly assholish advisors and ultimately vented their supreme frustrations by shooting their arrogant superiors in the head, repeatedly, using the various handguns they'd picked up on fieldtrips to Aurora Avenue.

Nick had imagined this scenario playing out in the Immunology offices for the better part of the year. There were one or two particularly despondent research associates, ones for whom Raj pulled no punches, and Nick had devised a series of appropriate responses, should they indeed go on the offensive one day, pumping Dr. Gupta full of hot lead, and, rather than turning the guns on themselves, decide to walk out of the hall and go on a shooting spree through the department offices.

Nick's proximity to ground zero for such an attack would be a double-edged sword. On the one hand, he'd be the first to know where the hail of gunfire was coming from, but at the same time, he'd also be the first person the gunman would see as he exited Raj's office. For this reason, when he arranged his cubicle, Nick had set his file cabinets and desk drawers in a layout which left about a foot and a half of space between the office furniture and the cubicle walls. At the first sign of trouble, he just had to slip to the floor and crawl back behind the equipment, leaving perhaps a foot or part of his leg exposed. He figured the shooter would either walk past without noticing him, or fire a few rounds into his legs, but leave his main body relatively sound. That's what he *hoped*. Anyway, he'd spent a great deal of time daydreaming about Raj's demise. Now it seemed relatively close, and even still, he didn't feel too sorry for the guy.

"You know your way around here, kid?" Luke asked.

"Yep."

From here it was a quick jaunt around the corner and down a flight of stairs into Raj's research wing.

"Then I guess it's showtime," Gomez said.

The two men raised their weapons and turned to Nick. Gomez pulled the radio from his shoulder and slipped it into Nick's hand.

"Wait here, kid," they said in unison.

Nick took a deep breath as the two men hesitated, then took off running around the corner. It seemed they had no sooner left him, than the sound of gunfire filled the air. He pulled his hands to his head, fighting the impulse to take off running down the corridor. A stray bullet tore through the sheetrock in the hallway, gypsum and plastic exploded into the air around him. Nick fell to the ground, pulling his arms and legs in for cover as the sound of the gunshots grew louder.

Then he heard the radio crackling to life.

Fuck. His ears were ringing. His eyes stung from concrete dust and debris. When he opened them, all he could see what a swirling dark blurr. He squeezed the transmitter on the radio again.

Christ.

"I'm gonna need some help up here."

The radio answered with static, then silence. Ransom pressed the button again as he rubbed at his eyes with his forearm. Whatever was in them was in there good.

"Repeat!" Ransom shouted. "I need back up."

"Where are you now?" Luke's voice shouted out at him as the sounds of gunfire echoed in the background.

"Eighth-floor landing," Ransom replied. "I was trying to cut through the hospital but got hit by one of those explosive sons of bitches they've rigged up on all the doors."

"Are you all right?"

"I'm blinded."

"Permanently?"

"I've got no idea!" Ransom shouted back.

The crackle of gunfire again, then Gomez's screaming voice.

"Luke's been hit! Luke's been hit!"

"Christ," Ransom muttered to himself. This was all just going great. "How bad?"

"In the leg. It went in and out," Gomez continued. "Kid,

where you at?"

"I'm here," Nick's voice answered hollowly.

"Can you get up to the roof?"

"No, that's a b-" Ransom started, then he was cut off.

"Yeah, I think so," Nick replied.

"Brick, I'm blocked off down here. They've got me cornered. I'm sending up the kid to be your eyes."

"Jesus," Brick thought . This goes wrong and I'll never gonna hear the end of it. He pulled himself upright and leaned his back against the wall. He picked up the handset again, pressed the button, and whispered into the phone. "Ten four, eighth-floor landing, kid."

The radio clicked, once more followed by the sound of bullets, then the air went dead.

"You better get here fast."

Each of the canisters was pressed securely in place on styrofoam packing boards, which were in turn strapped to the gurney that Jeff and his captors were carrying across the roof of the hospital. With the way this little WMD experiment had been produced and packaged, as though ready to be FedExed out to the field, Jeff couldn't help but wonder what Raj's final plans had been. Was he driven by revenge? Greed? Lust for power? He flashed back to an image of the cowardly little man standing there, holding one wrist in his hand.

Greed. That was the motive.

No question. One thing was certain. This had been anything but a routine project inspection. No walking in the door, listening to some arrogant professor's research spiel, trying to stay awake during yet another unbearable PowerPoint presentation, then faking a smile and nodding when the lights came up, and trying to feign interest once the reception was underway. No chuckling at jokes and conceits, mocking his own perceived stuffiness and wealth, while the whole time struggling to check out the bodies of the undergrad women around him. Those were the parties where the best-case scenario involved him going home with some nubile young female companion for the evening, and the worst-case scenario involved about four dozen operating-system jokes, or a witticism about the complexity of email. No, no, this had been a different sort of meeting altogether, and while those email barbs could get unbearably tedious, this particular scenario was its own kind of misery.

So what was his plan when they got to the copter?

He was in good shape.

He knew his way around a martial arts confrontation.

Would he just get to the copter, turn the tables on Simon, then Kung Fu it out with Tim? Would he get there, see his pilot, Mike, and through a series of winks and nods, iron out the logistics of their attack, perfectly coordinate their actions, and bada-bing, bada-boom, this would all be done?

That scenario seemed unlikely. For one thing, Jeff's communication skills were famously poor. He was better known for his indecipherable grunts and impatient hand motions than he was for the types of speeches and grand announcements that his more famous business partner and company co-founder had eventually become renowned. Besides, in shape or not, martial arts expert or not, he wasn't kidding himself; at heart he was a fifty-two-year-old former computer programmer, who, like all computer programmers, had a nerdy obsession with the martial arts, but that didn't mean he was at all cut out to square off against a couple of armed professionals, professionals who also happened to have some type of truly horrific weapon, several dozen of them actually, right at their disposal, within *arm's length,* to be precise.

They ran along the rooftop.

The sky was clear and sunny, but the wind was starting to pick up.

His arms were starting to ache under the weight of the canisters.

Just a little ways further and they'd be to the helipad, and then it would be showtime.

A gust of wind whipped his tie back and forth, and Jeff followed the motion of the fabric to the side, only to be distracted by the mass of people and vehicles swarming out across the campus up the hill from the medical center.

Was this on live TV?

Jesus.

He didn't want to die on live TV.

He'd have to stay focused. He'd have to get out of this successfully; otherwise he'd be the famous billionaire who bought the farm in a graceless show of incompetent self-defense, all on live TV, from chopper *FIVE* no less!

He'd better not split his pants.

They were at the end of the roof, where the building rose another two stories, and the only way up was by climbing a series of metal stairs that seemed to shoot straight up into the blue sky. No final destination, just air.

Course, he'd been up and down this ramp countless times before, the most recent time being, God, within the last few hours.

It seemed like days ago.

Maybe weeks.

Stop the maybes!

Decisive.

Action.

He'd get to the landing pad. They'd carry their load to the copter. Mike would be there. They'd radioed him to be ready. He'd open the door, he'd get out, they'd all start lifting in the gear, then Jeff would give him a look, Mike would know what to do, and they'd be in action, turning the tables on these motherfuckers.

That was the plan.

That was the *plan.*

Then they got to the helipad.

The copter was there.

His pilot was waiting.

"This is it," Jeff called to Tim, who glanced over his shoulder at him.

The doors to the copter were opening.

Jeff glanced at Simon, who seemed to be studying everything around him. Measuring the distance from one potential weapon or escape route to the next.

What an exhausting way to live.

Focus.

They got to the copter. The wind was really whipping around them now.

FOCUS!

The doors were opening, and Mike was walking out. Time for the head nod. The knowing exchange of glances. The pause, the briefest hesitation, before taking action.

His pilot was walking down the steps toward them.

Jeff looked down at the gurney they were carrying, shifting his hands under the weight, preparing to bend his knees, twist his body to the side, and heave the weight of it onto Simon's legs.

Only, that's when he looked up, and saw that the person coming towards him was not his pilot. It wasn't Mike. It was a man with a much sharper, harder looking face, one with darker, sunken eyes. Eyes that suddenly lifted, looked directly at him, held his gaze, and nodded at him ever so slightly.

Son of a bitch.

He was gonna have to do this. He was gonna have to try this kung fu shit on live TV.

He had better not split his pants.

Nick took the stairs two and three at a time. He felt the weight of the handgun in the pocket of his cargo pants. It banged against his thigh each time he took another leap upwards. He should pull it out, be ready for whatever he might encounter, but he was nervous about firing on the wrong person, or stumbling and setting the damn thing off -- some way to die. Instead of the hero, he'd be the asshole who fell and shot himself in the head.

Didn't that happen in a movie he'd seen recently?

Which one?

Hell, it didn't matter. He just didn't want to be that guy.

Course, just worrying about stumbling guaranteed that it

would happen, and it did.

At the landing to the seventh floor he grabbed the hand railing, started to spin himself around the corner and head up the next flight of stairs, but he caught his toe on the lowest step. His body sailed forward as his feet dragged behind. The famous sack of potatoes. He tried to slow his fall, grabbing at the railing at the last possible moment, but he went down harder. His shin and knee hit the concrete steps with a sudden, nauseating thump. He had a mental image of the bone inside turning bruised and purple.

Don't think about it.

Shake it off.

He got back on his feet, his leg screaming at him. Up another level, grab the rail, spin, and up again.

Then there he was.

Slumped against the wall in the middle of a mess of debris: Agent Ransom, who sat there, his gun held high, aimed directly at him.

Brick's eyes were half shut. They were red and running with tears, but the face behind the eyes didn't match. His expression was set, the features held in one cold, stony arrangement.

"Who. Goes. There?" Ransom asked.

"It's me."

"Oh good, the rescue squad."

Blood burped through Luke's fingers as he pressed them, clawlike, against the bloom of shredded skin that burst from the fabric of his pant leg. The pain was almost bearable at the moment, which scared him. He was probably in shock, or slipping into it very quickly. A pattern of bullets rippled the wall above his head, leaving the plaster and concrete torn to shit. Glass tinkled to the hospital floor around him.

Gomez stood just down the hall to the left side of the lab entrance; that was as far as he'd gotten since the assault began. Things had not gone smoothly, not from the get-go. They hadn't planned on going in firing, but that's how it had played out. Tim's, or rather *Griffin's* guys had been ready for them. The moment they set foot on the floor the bullets had come blasting through the glass, which made Gomez think that wired doorway had a bit more to it than just serving as the electrical match to a keg of dynamite. They must have had some sort of alarm hooked up, too.

Gomez pulled a two inch square mirror from his pocket, lifted it towards the door's shattered window, then turned it at an angle to catch a glimpse of the lab. He could see about seven guys in the front room, none of them wearing masks, all of them armed. At least two other figures paced the back room, training their guns on something, probably the hostages. Luke was down the hall from him, sitting under a six foot long window, circled by a fringe of glass shards. Luke looked at him and Gomez held up four fingers, once, then curled them in and opened three again. He jerked his thumb towards the window.

Luke nodded and held up three fingers.

Ten Guys.

Luke gave another nod, then he was on his feet, face screwed up in pain. He lifted his gun over the edge of the window and fired off seven rounds - aimed, fired, aimed, fired - then he hit the floor again.

Gomez spun up to his feet, aiming through the door's broken glass, firing shots at the three remaining figures. Either the others had been hit, or they'd hit the deck. A wise move.

Boom!

The first shot hit one of the men in the side of the neck, slicing through the tendon that kept his head from wobbling free. It wobbled, and blood sprayed out like ketchup from a diner bottle.

Gomez fired again.

The second shot took off the guy's head.

A twist of the gun and a turn to the left, and the next shot hit a second guy square in the face.

By the time the gun had turned again, the third man was gone.

Smart guy.

The glass crunched under Luke's bloody boot as he stood again, the muzzle of his weapon once more pivoting on the window's edge. He waited, leaning his weight against his right shoulder, which he pressed into the wall for support. He angled his rifle up and over the edge of the window, spraying the floor inside with a shower of bullets. Then he hazarded a look inside and damn near lost his head for the trouble. Three bullets tore through the wall beside him-

Thoom thoom thoom!

Gomez dove to the other side of the door, glass tinkling against his leg, one piece slicing through his pant leg and ripping into the flesh. He clenched his teeth, shuffled to the bottom left corner of the window, then bobbed up.

Bam! Bam!

He hit the guy in the corner of the left eye. Bullet hit bone hit eye, and **POP**, the whole side of the guy's face ruptured and rippled down the front, even as the next bullet whizzed through the mass of falling flesh and blood, and ripped into the guy's throat, sending his arms and leg shooting straight out to the sides as he fell backwards, stiff as a board.

Gomez dove to the floor as another man emerged from behind a lab bench. Gomez aimed, fired, and got him perfectly. Like his associate before him, the man's arms and legs went straight out to the sides as a spatter of blood bloomed at the center of his forehead, exactly at the point where Luke fired another single, clean shot.

Thoop.

The body tumbled to the floor and the room fell silent.

Gomez sat on the ground, breathing deeply.

Luke was crouched on one knee, shaking from the adrenaline. He lowered himself to the floor, propping his body up with one arm.

Then the door in the back of the lab opened, and one by one, men and women dressed in lab coats and carrying backpacks began filing out. They murmured softly to one another, their voices barely whispers, many of them uttering only prayers.

Luke turned to Gomez, his brow crimped in the middle.

Gomez lifted a hand to shield the glare from an overhead light that now dangled from the ceiling, spinning a lazy fluorescent twirl in the draft from the ventilation system. He looked past the crowd moving out of the lab, now filing out into the hallway, and through the crowd he could just make out the figure of a little man. A man with a moustache and a tense, drawn-up body, who stood near the door of the backroom, holding a canister in his hands and shouting something to three more gunmen, who stood in the back corner, their guns slung over their shoulders, their hands raised in the air.

The little figure turned to the doorway to see the progress of the captives as they slipped away to freedom; then he redirected his attention to the men in the back, and lifted the canister a bit closer to his chest.

They made it through the rest of the building without incident. At least, without Ransom setting any more explosives off in his own face. Since Nick had banged his leg up on the stairs, and since a blinded Brick was something less than agile and quick, the trip through the medical facilities could be looked at as one *long* incident. But, they had made it. In the main tower they found a functioning elevator and they took it. They were in the elevator now, rising swiftly up to the roof, perhaps a bit *too* swiftly for Nick's comfort. The doors would open at any moment, and more likely than not, they'd be dead center in the middle of the action.

"Don't shit yourself, kid."

Nick looked at him. "Don't blind yerself, pops."

Brick smirked. "Getting fresh. I like that."

There was silence.

"I didn't mean that in a, you know, sexual way," Ransom added.

"Jesus," Nick muttered. "I know."

The floors dinged by.

"You been to this landing pad before? Do you know the

layout?"

"Nope," Nick replied.

"Great. Well, I guess just get your gun ready, and we'll make it up as we go along."

"Same plan as usual then." Nick said.

"Yep. Oh, and kid, this could get a little crazy. Try not to go apeshit with that gun of yours."

Nick took a deep breath.

Bing.

Nick and Ransom lifted their weapons as if on cue.

Nick watched the joint between the two metal doors. Light glowed dully on the brushed-metal surface. Then the doors pulled open with a wheeze. Sunlight streamed inside and the roar of a helicopter engine engulfed them.

Ransom blinked his bleary eyes.

"Shit, it's bright out here!"

"That mean you can see?"

"Hardly."

Nick took a cautious step out of the elevator, which opened onto a covered metal platform. A series of metal stairs climbed up from the platform to a catwalk above, which then crossed over to a raised platform. From the sound of the helicopter rotors above, and the gusts of air roaring over the edge and down over them, it appeared they'd come to the right location.

"Can you at least make it up some stairs?" Nick shouted in Ransom's ear.

Ransom nodded.

Nick grabbed the man's shoulder, leading him towards the metal railing. Ransom put his hand on the metal bar, feeling his way onward. Nick took the first steps up, glancing back at Ransom as he slowly followed behind.

Nick held his gun at the ready, hoping to God he'd flipped off the safety. At the top of the stairs, he got a clear, but somewhat protected view of the helicopter as it sat on the platform. The side door was open, and he could just make out the figures of two people inside, along with two other men still standing on the landing pad. They were loading something into the main cabin. Metal containers of some kind. There were dozens of them.

"Can you see 'em?" Ransom asked.

"Yeah, they're loading something."

"Metal canisters?"

"Yeah, how'd you-"

"Shit," Ransom said. "Who all is there?"

"Two gunmen, a pilot, and a guy in a torn-up suit."

"Don't hit the guy in the suit, whatever you do!"

"And what are we doing?"

"No idea, kid. They look like they're taking off?"

"They're fixing to," Nick said matter of factly.

No sooner did Ransom speak, than all hell broke loose on the platform.

***

Jeff was totally thrown by the sudden appearance of this stranger as he worked in the cabin to secure the canisters. He'd planned for a much different scenario, one in which he knew the character and motives of his accomplice, his right-hand man (in the air at least), Mike. Now there was this new guy in the pilot's uniform, clearly a fed, who gave him a weak nod, which briefly comforted Jeff, until he realized that any misguided heroics would get them all killed.

Maybe this guy worked with Tim and Simon, but most likely he didn't. From the subtle flash in the man's eye, and his way of observing Jeff's captors, Jeff guessed the guy was FBI. From what he'd seen and heard in the past, he figured the presence of this stranger in his midst gave him at best a 50/50 chance of survival. Maybe that was the best he could hope for under these conditions.

He'd been put in the cabin first thing, and now he sat in a chair, calmly observing the situation.

Tim's man and the pilot were quietly loading the last of the canisters , which, along with their Styrofoam padding, were fitting perfectly in the walkway between the back seats. Jeff stole a peek at them as Tim conferred with the pilot.

Next thing he knew, they were preparing for takeoff.

That's when everything changed.

The pilot closed the main cabin door, then walked around the side of the aircraft. He had just opened the door to climb inside, when Tim lifted his handgun and fired two shots into the man's chest. The pilot was thrown backward, pulsating in the air, once to the left and once to the right. The man stumbled backwards, tripping over the landing skid and landing on his back with a thud.

Tim climbed into the copter and locked the cabin door behind him.

"Friend of yours?" Tim asked.

Jeff shook his head. "Never seen him before in my life."

Nevertheless, lets play it safe," Tim responded, before

reaching over and fastening Jeff's wrist to his seat arm with a thin pair of handcuffs.

***

Raj was shouting something, but his excitement, combined with his poor mastery of the English language, made translating and comprehension difficult. From where Luke and Gomez were standing, they could see him, his moustache dancing like a corpulent lip-dwelling caterpillar, shouting to the men with their arms raised at the far end of the room.

"Don't move! Don't move! Don't move!" he rattled off.

The men stood frozen in place.

"You move and I flip the switch," Raj continued, raising the canister for emphasis as the last of the hostages squeezed past him.

"Hurry!" he shouted to the group. "Hurry."

Men, women, students, all went past him, some casting an appreciative look in his direction, others lost in their own worlds of panic and shock.

Raj's fingers slipped on the edge of the canister. He glanced down at his hands. He had never set one of these things off personally. Hopefully the diagrams his lab flunkies had prepared for publication had been accurate. His hands went cold and clammy at the realization of what was happening. He looked around, then looked at the faces of the gunmen on the other side of the room.

What was he planning to do?

What had he been *thinking* would *happen* all this time?

Nothing good could ever have come from this bastardized research.

This wasn't *science*. This wasn't an *experiment*.

This was weapon building.

This was *terrorism*.

The last of the hostages walked past him. Raj felt the panic of a passenger racing to leap into the last dinghy on a sinking ship.

One of the gunmen locked eyes with him.

Raj recognized him suddenly. This guy had been one of his lab techs last year. He'd been hired 'cause he worked cheap, for next to nothing, save for a work visa.

Raj sighed. Guess his accountant had been right. It never pays to be cheap, something in the long haul always comes back to bite you in the ass!

"Close the door," Raj said softly.

The man nodded and pulled it closed behind him.

The other gunmen started for their weapons as Raj flipped the switch on the canister.

He started walking towards them.

From where Luke and Gomez were standing, they saw only a whirlwind of confusion as the gunmen lifted their weapons and opened fire. Raj was hit in the shoulder and chest, blood spraying out in puffs of pink vapor. Then, in a brief slow-motion hiccup of time, the metal canister in his hands erupted, sending out a cloud of gas. Just as quickly as it happened, the windows of the back room were covered in blood.

The room fell silent.

"Let's get these people out of here," Luke whispered.

Gomez pulled his hands from his eyes, shaken, and nodded his head slowly.

***

Murray fell from the helicopter, hitting the ground hard.

The bullets had broken at least two of his ribs, but hell, he was still thankful for the government vest, and glad that Halliburton hadn't gotten *all* of the government's last equipment contracts. He lifted his head to look up, but the wind had been knocked out of him. He gulped for air, seeing stars and flickering images as the door on the copter swung closed. He watched through the glass as Tim climbed over to the controls.

Inside the cabin, things were really getting interesting.

"Close the doors," Tim shouted to Simon.

Simon stood, preparing to follow orders.

Nick stood around the edge of the stairs, describing the scene to Ransom.

"The pilot's down."

"I think my vision's coming back," Ransom responded.

"Can you see what's happening?"

"Someone's coming out of the copter!" Ransom shouted, lifting his gun suddenly.

"Caref-" Nick started, but was cut off by the sounds of Brick's handgun.

BLAM! BLAM! BLAM!

Three gunshots rang out.

The first bullet flew past Simon's ear, ripping into the headrest of the front passenger seat.

Simon spun to the side and down as the next shot ricocheted off the side of the copter's frame.

The third bullet hit Jeff Pepper in his left shoulder. Jeff winced in pain, trying to pull his hand up to the wound, but his wrist was strapped to the armrest.

"Stop!" Nick shouted. "You just hit Pepper!"

Brick's heart sank. "Is he okay?"

"He's still moving. But yeah, you hit him."

Brick raised his gun again. "He knows me, it'll be okay."

Nick put his hands on Ransom's arm, shaking his head.

"Someone's firing on us!" Simon shouted. "Get us in the air!"

Tim shook his head furiously from side to side. The sounds of the engines changed pitch as the blades shifted their angle and the copter's skids lifted away from the platform. Simon moved for the doors as two more shots rang out, neither one of them hitting the copter as it twisted in the air.

The copter started moving faster.

Up, up.

The landing pad below moved away in jerky twists and lunges.

"You trying to knock me out of the fucking thing?" Simon shouted to Tim.

"It's been a while," Tim screamed back.

The chopper pulled clear of the building, the platform disappearing from Jeff's sightline as the ground 12 stories below moved into his frame of vision. Simon stepped toward the edge of the cabin. His hand reached out for the door handle, just as Jeff leapt up from his seat and pivoted to the side, throwing his hip around, and with it his foot, which spun out in a wide arc, hitting Simon squarely in the back. The man fell forward, out of the helicopter, and into free air.

The copter lurched to the side as Tim looked back to see what had happened.

Simon's arms pinwheeled in the air. He locked eyes with Jeff as he seemed to hang in place momentarily. Then he turned, just as his head caught a sharp whack from the helicopter skid.

Jeff saw the man's eyes go dead, even before his body plunged like a rock to the ground below.

Tim lifted his gun, firing at Jeff, who crouched to the floor as two bullets flew wildly astray, one hitting the back of the passenger seat, the other shooting straight out of the cabin.

Nick and Ransom watched from below as the chopper circled back toward the building in a swooping turn, the pilot barely maintaining control.

"What the fuck is going on in there?" Ransom shouted.

"It's coming back at us! What should I do?" Nick screamed.

"Get ready to duck!"

The engine sputtered and whirred, threatening to stall.

In the cabin, Tim again spun around to fire at Jeff, who tried his best to stick close to the floor, even as the handcuffs held his hand fast to the armrest. His other arm was throbbing now, the coat sleeve growing a deep crimson as blood from the bullet wound bled through the fabric.

Will was going to be pissed!

The fear of his valet's wrath gave Jeff a boost of energy.

He leapt to his feet, lunging towards Tim in an awkward repeat of his previous, highly successful kick. This time his foot glanced off the back of the front seat, deflecting slightly, but still hitting Tim in the wrist, sending the handgun flying free, where it hit the side of the cabin and slid out of reach. Tim recoiled in pain, the chopper again swirling out of control as it swooped back and forth over the roof of the hospital.

The movement knocked Jeff from his feet. He fell backwards awkwardly, his restrained arm wrenching his shoulder as the weight of his body crashed down. He looked down, realizing he was laid out on the flat of silver canisters. Their shiny metal bodies shimmered in the whirling daylight. Jeff reached out to them with his injured arm even as Tim regained control of the chopper, sending the machine lurching from side to side.

The door to the cabin swung open, and Jeff's feet slid briefly out into the open air before he caught the bottom of the seat support with his foot. He reached out farther and farther for the canisters.

Tim saw what he was doing and sent the aircraft into wilder and wilder in-air acrobatics.

Then Jeff's fingertips brushed the nearest canisters. His index and middle fingers made contact with the switches, flipping them up with a satisfying electronic *ping*. Blue lights lit up on the metal bodies. No sooner did the flashes of blue light up his face, than Jeff was sliding across the cabin floor again.

The copter tilted to the side, and Jeff was suddenly airborne. But his flight was brief.

Snap.

The handcuff caught his wrist, catching him before he fell. The wrist snapped, twisting and splintering at a terribly improper angle, even as it held him in place.

Nick watched as Jeff dangled from the side of the copter

as it spun wildly. The pilot was trying to shake Jeff out of the aircraft.

Murray jumped to his feet as the copter swung down toward the platform, its skids coming within inches of the surface, then shooting back up into the air.

Jeff's legs kicked wildly. Shouts of pain, panic, and anger roared from his mouth.

Murray ran for the edge of the platform, pulled a gun from the back pocket of his vest, and aimed for the handcuff chain that clasped Jeff's wrist to the arm of the passenger chair. He fired two shots, both of which missed their mark as the chopper again spun toward him. Murray ducked, rolling to the side and over the edge of the building towards the next roof level below. He hit the surface with a thud, knocked out from the impact.

"What's happening now?" Ransom asked.

"Pepper's dangling from the side of the chopper!" Nick shouted.

"Handcuffs?"

"I assume! Sure as hell doesn't look like he's there on purpose."

"Can you hit 'em?"

"What?"

"The cuffs! Can you hit 'em?"

Nick turned to him. "Hell, I can try."

"Do it!"

***

Fuck, this hurt.

Jeff's wrist was screaming bloody murder.

His arm was howling like a banshee.

His body was flailing wildly in the air, exerting all the more pressure on his totaled arm and wrist.

Plus -- his eyes locked on the twinkling blue lights -- these fucking canisters, whatever the hell they were, were ready to go off any second. The lights racing around the switches were going round and round in faster and faster rotations. He didn't know much about these things, but his hunch was that that was not good.

Tim gripped the controls, rocking the aircraft from side to side, trying to tip the platter of canisters out of the cabin. He was having no such luck, but he was sure as hell coming close to tearing Jeff's arm from its socket.

Each time the chopper listed down to the right side, Jeff flailed his arms and legs, trying to get a foothold on the skid or the side of the cabin. When it went back in the other direction, Jeff slammed into the side, his body hitting the metal shell with a jolt, the momentum spinning him around.

To make things worse, the view below was a helter-skelter nightmare -- moving back and forth from rooftop to the freefall possibility of nothing but air. Each time the helicopter, with Jeff dangling from the side, appeared over the edge of the building, he could hear the crowd gasp. He just bet the news crews were having a field day with this. It wasn't every day the world's third richest man, the *software* guy, got battered around like this on live television.

Oh, and to make matters worse, he'd been shot by his old *high school buddy,* Brick Ransom. In the instant before the first shot hit him in the shoulder, Jeff had caught a glimpse of his old friend on the rooftop, taking dazed, rather half-assed aim at

Simon, and instead hitting him.

Now he was in this predicament.

Christ, if he survived this, the footage of this moment would be in every news bio, video tribute toast, and *Saturday Night Live* sketch from now until the day he died. Hopefully that would come later than sooner! Christ! Hell, let them air this shit whenever the hell they wanted to! Just let him get two feet back on the fucking ground!

The copter was banking south of the building towards Lake Union. Jeff's leg movements had slowed, probably from exhaustion.

Nick held the gun aloft, closed one eye, and took slow, steady aim at the chain above the Pepper's wrist.

He'd get one shot.

One shot, then the pilot would pull away from that building, away from all the gunfire.

Nick tracked the movement, sweeping his arm to the side, moving the view up and down as the body of the aircraft continued its topsy turvy movements. The aircraft moved over the edge of the building, its engine seeming to sputter and wheeze. Then it started back over the rooftop, and Nick pulled the trigger.

Kuh-pshow!

The chain around Jeff's wrist let go. Completely. One minute he was flying backwards, over the roof. The next he was falling through thin air as the chopper hurtled away, over the edge, over the crowd, to the north of the building. Jeff looked up into the copter's cabin as he hung in the air, briefly motionless. He locked eyes with Tim as the man struggled at the controls, then held still, his face going slack.

Behind Tim, in the middle of the cabin, a flash of explosive went off, and a cloud of mist filled the air around him. Jeff watched in horrific curiosity to see what would happen. For a moment it seemed nothing would, then Tim's eyes seemed to bug out, the whites swelling out of his eyelids. His face and cheeks puffed out in a ghastly expression of surprise, as Tim's now swollen hands flew up to his neck in panic. Blood seeped from Tim's eyes as Jeff regained his sense of gravity and began pinwheeling his arms and legs. Still, he looked inside the cabin, saw the burst of blood from Tim's nose and ears, saw the mist of pink vapor burst from the man's eyes and mouth. Then he saw the worst of it, the final hiccup, as the man's body seemed to twist inside out, erupting in a geyser of blood and tissue as the glass on the front of the helicopter was covered in blood.

Then, Jeff fell towards the rooftop. He twisted his body in the air, trying to direct the impact to his back, turn into it a little. Closer, closer, the rooftop flew up at his face as he hurtled downward.

Bam!

He landed with a thud at the edge of the platform, the force of the impact sending him flying head over heels toward the ledge, before he stopped, his head and shoulders hanging over the side. He reached out to hold himself in place, his broken wrist on one side, his wounded arm on the other. He closed his eyes in pain, and took a deep breath. When he looked up, a young man, 25, 26, was standing over him, reaching out his hand. Jeff took it, and grunted as the guy pulled him forward, up and away from the edge. He struggled to his feet, dazed, as he heard the sound of his helicopter's wheezing, gasping, sputtering engine. The two of them looked over at the chopper as it whirled about wildly, its dead pilot's ruptured remains slumped at the controls.

The chopper began making wider and ever wilder movements, spinning toward the corner of the building with its rotors. Jeff watched, fascinated, until the young man again pulled on his arm, rather forcefully, leading him towards the metal stairs and away from the platform.

Then the chopper's nose tilted down as it hugged the top of the building and rocketed away towards the lake. Its flight was cut short as the rotor blades made contact with the roof, clipping their tips on the concrete surface, and sending shards of metal blasting outwards like an abstract porcupine. Jeff and Nick dove for the stairs and shrapnel screamed through the air around them. When they looked up, the body of the mortally wounded aircraft was hurtling forward, over the edge of the building, in a listing arc, still headed for the lake. The sound faded away as their eyes bulged.

The machine seemed to hover in the air. Then it moved farther and farther away, off into the distance, over the crowd below, over the buildings of the south campus, and out towards the water, where it quietly and gracefully splashed down in an oddly muted crash landing.

The twisted, burning wreckage floated in place for a moment, bobbing on the surface, before slipping beneath the waves and disappearing from sight.

***

The bomb squad disarmed the triggers on the doors, and slowly but surely the people trapped inside the building tumbled out, some running to their friends, who stood at the edge of the crowd, others stumbling out into the fading evening light, their expressions dazed, their eyes half-shut from fatigue, and fear, and exhaustion.

It took the crowd a few moments to notice Ransom, Jeff, and Nick once they finally made their way from the building. Jeff's shirt was soaked through with blood. He was limping, his leg injured from his pinwheeling exit from the doomed aircraft. Nick was also struggling to walk. The two of them stumbled along together, balancing out each other's weight, their gaits resembling the strides of geriatrics in a senior citizen three-legged race.

Ransom followed behind, blinking as his vision slowly returned. No sooner did the crowd recognize them and pinpoint Jeff, than the three of them were surrounded by a mob of cameramen, TV news crews, and pure noise.

Flashes started popping in their faces.

Ransom squinted through bleary eyes as the cameras moved in closer and the voices of reporters and well wishers came at them from all sides.

"We've got an injured man here," Ransom shouted to the crowd. "Step aside, we've got an injured man here."

Then the crowd parted, sliced down the middle by Sam Ballard and several of his men, who wheeled a gurney between them.

"Out of the way!" Sam shouted. "Out of the way!"

Two of the firefighters, along with Ransom and Nick, helped Jeff up onto the edge of the gurney, where he sat for a moment, catching his breath before they leaned him onto his back and rolled him towards a waiting ambulance.

He was immediately swamped by EMTs, who sliced off his shirt, checked his vitals, pressed on his wounds, and got him ready to go.

Jeff saw everything through a haze, suddenly slipping into shock from what had happened.

No, he thought, I can't do this.

Mind over matter.

Sensei will be displeased.

Just before he closed his eyes, Jeff rolled his head to one side and saw the stand-in for the pilot, Murray, sitting on a stoop on the side of the road, holding an ice pack to his head as an EMT brought him water. Jeff blinked his eyes and lifted his hand to get the man's attention, then he rolled onto his back and had just enough time to see Nina step into his field of view, her expression worried, but as always, authoritative.

"Where are you taking him?" she demanded.

"Right up the street," someone answered.

"Well, good," Nina responded. "They're the best."

"I know we are."

Then she walked over to Jeff, put her hand on his shoulder, and climbed in the ambulance along with him as they loaded him up and closed the doors.

***

The bodies were hard to watch.

They came out slowly, each in a white zippered bag.

The workers tried to make each one's removal quiet and dignified, not to announce each new discovery, but every time a new gurney rolled through the crowd, or agents emerged with another body bag, the news crew went wild trying to get footage.

Nick sat at the edge of the crowd, watching the latest bags being carried from the building. Were some of them the gunmen? Probably. Were some of them students? He didn't know. One of them was Renoir, he knew that now. He'd heard some of the agents speaking to an older woman earlier, who'd seemed strong right up until the end, when she grew quiet, pulled in her arms and legs, and without a sound, or a word, leaned forward and crumpled in on herself as the people around her caught her and carried her away. Nick recognized the woman as Renoir's wife.

All around him, people were hugging their loved ones, calling their families, or sitting alone, staring off into space. Survivor's shock.

For a moment, Nick thought of calling Kendra, telling her that he was all right -- assuming she hadn't seen anything on TV about the event -- but in his heart, whether he thought she'd be concerned or not, he knew he wouldn't call. That was over, and it was time that it was resolved. The last of their strained phone conversations had revealed a pretty blatant subtext. They were in love, just not with each other. Each of them sensed that the other was with someone else. Nick had no allusions of

Kendra returning to him, and he sensed that she was feeling the same way.

He made his way out of the front entryway, to the treatment center that had been set up by the curb, where he was greeted by the EMTs and led over to the concrete steps along the exterior of the courtyard. They told him to sit down and relax while his body gathered itself together.

All Nick could do was picture a face and a feeling, hair and lips and eyes, and *her*.

Yes, he had thought of his wife, of Kendra, but she wasn't the person he wanted to see. Who he *needed* to see. He *needed* someone else.

Then he looked up and saw her coming through the crowd. She was looking for *him*.

Morgan.

***

Onion tartlet.

He had to keep reminding himself.

He had something good going for him, someone else, someone who might be more than a bit forthcoming tonight, especially after he made her his special meal.

"Onion tartlet," Brick muttered to himself.

"What was that, Ransom?" Aftab turned and asked.

Onion tartlet.

"Nothin'."

He was watching Morgan and that kid Nick. Goofy guy was all thumbs and elbows. She was pure leg and heart. A vitalic little nymph. A love fawn. An intimate biscuit. Or something. Dammit. He was punchy, and jealous.

Jealous of two kids in their twenties.

But how could he not be, she was *gorgeous*. A fantasy come to life.

A fantasy.

Then again, so was Victoria. She had killer arms, and legs, and lips, and hair, and she had one thing more, *experience*. Oh, and once she'd had his onion tartlet she'd be all but melting for him. Melting.

He ran through the rest of the recipe in his mind. Then he glanced at his watch. If he headed home now, he could just get things together in time. He could just barely put the finishing touches on dinner, slip the main dish in the oven, and get everything ready to slip in between the sheet.

The lovebirds let go of each other for a moment. Nick looked over at Ransom and nodded. Ransom nodded back. The he turned and walked over to a Seattle squad car, flashed them his badge, and asked for a ride home.

***

After they'd answered all the authorities' questions, Nick and Morgan went to Nick's place.

They went to *Nick's place*.

That was a first. In all the excitement of janitorial closets and university back rooms, the two of them had never been together in Nick's own bed.

The next day they slept. And slept. Holding each other tightly as morning sunlight streamed in through the curtains, reflecting off the sheets and softly lighting their faces.

Then the phone rang. Nick rolled over and felt around for it in the mass of dirty laundry piled around the bed. He brought the receiver to his mouth and answered it.

"Hello?"

"Yes," a woman's voice replied. "I'm trying to reach Nick."

"Speaking," Nick answered as he wiped sleep from his eyes.

"My name is Nina Parker. I'm an associate of Jeff Pepper's."

"Oh," Nick sat up suddenly. "How can I help you?"

"We have a proposal for you. Mr. Pepper has been getting a lot of calls from publishers. Everyone wants a book deal with him, they want to put out something on everything that's happened."

"Okay?" Nick replied.

Nina continued, "In learning more about the people involved, including yourself and Mr. Ransom, Jeff's friend from the FBI, we learned that you're an editor at the University."

"I was. Not sure there's anyone left for me to work for."

"Well, we also got a look at some of your college transcripts. From the look of your thesis, we're guessing the last thing you wanted to be doing was editing research papers, right?"

Before he could answer, Nina responded for him.

"Of course not. Which is why Jeff, I mean Mr. Pepper, thought you might like to write this book with him."

Nick said nothing.

"Nick?"

"Yes." Nick said.

" That's pretty much our proposal. What should I tell him?"

Nick looked over at Morgan, who rolled over next to him.

"Yes, tell him yes. Absolutely," Nick replied.

"I'm glad to hear that," Nina said. "Jeff will be thrilled."

Morgan lifted one leg under the sheets, bringing it up over Nick's body.

"Okay," Nick whispered.

"We'll be in touch with the paperwork this week."

Morgan raised herself up, the sheets falling away from her body as she straddled him.

"Great," Nick responded, and slipped the phone back in its cradle.

He looked up at Morgan, wrapped his arms around her, and they started again.

Acknowledgments

Thank you to Jason Croatto for the snazzy new cover art and interior layout!

Thanks to Elizabeth Attebery for cleaning up the text and pointing out where my dislike for some of the book's more dastardly fictional characters might have gotten the better of me.

Thanks to all the websites that spread the word about this book online.

I can't forget the help of my editorial assistants, Bueller and Mimi and their sisters Winter and Mocha, who have all provided welcome entertainment and amusement as I poured over the text of this book throughout the years.

And of course, thanks my wife Stephanie, who has put up with me for 13 years now, and didn't throw me out on the street when horrible jobs, silly excuses, and plenty of frustration undoubtedly made me an absolute monster to live with. She's also fairly patient when it comes to the way I obsess about, well, everything.

Thank you to Paul Esmond for the excellent photograph for the back of the book.

Mike Attebery earned a Bachelor of Fine Arts Degree from the School of Film and Animation at the Rochester Institute of Technology. When he isn't writing or editing books and screenplays, Mike spends his days worrying about... everything, and kicking and knocking on stuff to see what it's made out of. He lives in Seattle, Washington with his wife and their two ferrets, Winter and Mocha. He is currently at worked on his fourth novel.

www.mikeattebery.com

Printed in the USA
CPSIA information can be obtained
at www.ICGtesting.com
LVHW041557030324
773431LV00001B/79

9 780615 591438